THE NARROWS OF FEAR
(WAPAWIKOSCIKANIK)

We gratefully acknowledge the support of the Canada Council for the Arts and the Ontario Arts Council for our publishing program. We also acknowledge the financial support of the Government of Canada.

Front cover artwork: Carol Rose GoldenEagle, "Our Stolen Sisters," 2011, acrylic on canvas and mixed media, 48 x 36 inches.

Cover design: Val Fullard

The Narrows of Fear (Wapawikoscikanik) is a work of fiction. All the characters portrayed in this book are fictitious and any resemblance to persons living or dead is purely coincidental.

Library and Archives Canada Cataloguing in Publication

Title: The narrows of fear (wapawikoscikanik) : a novel / Carol Rose GoldenEagle. Other titles: Wapawikoscikanik
Names: GoldenEagle, Carol Rose, 1963– author.
Series: Inanna poetry & fiction series.
Description: Series statement: Inanna poetry & fiction series
Identifiers: Canadiana (print) 20200330608 | Canadiana (ebook) 20200330691 | ISBN 9781771337892 (softcover) | ISBN 9781771337908 (epub) | ISBN 9781771337915 (Kindle) | ISBN 9781771337922 (pdf) Subjects: LCGFT: Novels.
Classification: LCC PS8607.A5567 N37 2020 | DDC C813/.6—dc23

Printed and bound in Canada

Inanna Publications and Education Inc.
210 Founders College, York University
4700 Keele Street, Toronto, Ontario, Canada M3J 1P3
Telephone: (416) 736-5356 Fax: (416) 736-5765
Email: inanna.publications@inanna.ca   Website: www.inanna.ca

THE NARROWS OF FEAR
(WAPAWIKOSCIKANIK)

a novel

Carol Rose GoldenEagle

Inanna poetry & fiction series

INANNA PUBLICATIONS AND EDUCATION INC.
TORONTO, CANADA

WARNING: Contains scenes of sexual, physical, and psychological violence

*Dedicated to Bev—my friend & sister,
their Auntie—our love always
and to strong Indigenous women
everywhere across Turtle Island*

ALSO BY CAROL ROSE (DANIELS) GOLDENEAGLE

FICTION
Bear Skin Diary
Bone Black

POETRY
Hiraeth

Grief doesn't always begin as a process that is the result of the death of a Loved One. Sometimes, grief begins as a result of a broken heart and that usually never ends. But, moment by moment, you learn to treat your heart more delicately than ever before. And eventually, grief turns into strength. It is then that your heart warms the sun and your hugs are healing and your story becomes the truth.

—Words of advice from a friend

PART I
THE SINS OF MAN

1. MELTING

THE INTERIOR OF GABRIEL'S ICE FISHING SHACK has looked the same since the day the Old Man pounded together these mismatched pieces of wood. At seventy years of age, only a bit of arthritis has slowed Gabriel down. His strong arms and body are still fit to chop wood and go out hunting on the land as often as possible.

Inside the shack, Gabriel has drilled four holes into the ice. Each of them are about twelve inches wide. There is one at each corner of the small structure that has a couple of ridiculously small windows—enough to let in the sunlight, but not large enough to fit someone intent on breaking in. The shack wears a plain plywood façade and interior so as not to call attention to itself.

Gabriel's son, Maynard, should feel safe here. He does not want to call attention either to himself, or to his thoughts. He's started to grow a braid but his hair is at that awkward length—not yet long enough to pull back out of his face, but too long to keep tidy when he wears it loose . Old Gabriel has been teasing him, saying he looks like a girl.

The two sit in peaceful silence for most of the day until the Old Man says the same thing he's said a thousand times over the years. "Slow today, my boy. Papiyataki-kisikaw. This one was our honey hole yesterday. Caught five perch."

Maynard nods in agreement. Small talk. It can be comforting or suffocating.

Neither of them anticipates hearing a knock. Usually, anyone approaching the shack can be heard long before they reach the door. But today's wind makes the ice and the travel of sound unpredictable.

Old Gabriel automatically thinks the worst, "Likely a Conservation Officer. What the hell? Don't they know we have Treaty Rights?" It takes him all of ten seconds to open the door. He is greeted by a howling wind and a clean-shaven young man who is no older than twenty. A monias. White skin. Reddish hair.

The young man introduces himself as Shad and tells them his family has a cabin on the lake—a cabin that's been in his family for decades. Started out as a simple plywood shack too. "I just love coming out here," young Shad admits, "truly feels like I can talk to God when I am by myself on this landscape." He smiles at Maynard, "I am pretty sure you know what I mean."

Shad tells them he is on the ice today working as an entrepreneur. Gabriel spies the contraption that the polite young man has attached to his sled. Shad explains. "Seems to me that ice fishing can get someone off their usual routine of eating. You are out here all day. Probably missed breakfast. So I came up with a solution. My meals on wheels—if you want to call it that." With this Shad recites what he's brought, "I have hot coffee and tea. Hot dogs and ham sandwiches. And a couple flavours of potato chips."

The price is right. Fifty cents for the hot beverages and a dollar for the hot dogs and sandwiches. Neither of them eat chips. The Old Man speaks, "You're just damn lucky today, my young friend. Normally, I do not bring cash out here on the ice. What would be the reason? But we'll take two hot dogs with mustard and two hot tea. Three dollars, right?"

Shad nods in agreement, just as one of the rods down the honey hole starts to jiggle.

"Holy, first one all day. You must be a good luck charm." Gabriel reels in a large pickerel. Must weigh two pounds.

Meantime, Shad hands a warm hot dog to Gabriel. He pauses for a moment before giving Maynard his dog. "You want anything extra with that—other than mustard? I have some cheese." Maynard declines and takes the hot dog as offered.

But what else is going on?

Maynard doesn't expect to feel warmth when the heel of his hand touches the raw skin of the handsome stranger. It's because the warmth he feels extends to his groin. It frightens Maynard and he looks away—making small talk again about the honey hole that brought up a colossal fish. "Those cheeks would likely add some flavour to this dog." He jokes with his Dad, purposely so because in turning his attention to Gabriel, it forces him to break eye contact with the young visitor.

Gabriel laughs, "I suppose, eh? Hey, what is it they say about how hot dogs are made?"

Shad laughs too. Whether he gets the joke or not doesn't matter. A good salesman always agrees with his customer. "My family is out here at the cabin for the next week and a bit. Maybe I'll see you again. I'm trying to raise some money for a trip to Cuba."

"Well then, I'll make sure to always bring some coin." Gabriel takes a bite of his hot dog, mustard squishing onto his index finger and thumb. "And thanks again. It's a while until supper." He looks at Maynard, and adds, "I think we have enough to make a nice chowder tonight. Even with just this one fish. Hope Sandy loves it too."

With that Shad waves goodbye and fires up his snowmobile. He estimates there are sixty other fishing shacks occupying the ice today. That's a lot of hot dogs.

2. COMING HOME

THE RADIO ANNOUNCER DRONES ON. "We are sorry about last night. We predicted it would be clear, warm, and sunny today, but we were wrong. Today's forecast calls for cloudy skies and the possibility of snow...."

Wrong again! Sandy mutters as she throws a checkered woolen blanket to the back seat of her Jeep Wrangler. It is an updated model from her old Jeep that Sandy traded in at the beginning of the new year: "New beginnings, new pony." She continues to mutter to herself. "I always like to give my vehicle a name. Hmmm. What will I call this one?" She is leaning towards the name Sadie. It is a variation on the name Sarah, which means princess. The reason for Sadie? Because of Cinderella and her coach bringing the fairy tale character back to safety before any secrets were discovered.

Her new Jeep is black in colour, like the old one. Sandy still feels the need to mask herself in shadow, hiding from things unseen when daylight turns to night. Why does she feel this way? No idea. Bad habit.

She checks her watch. It is eight a.m. Even with good weather northern roadways in winter are tenuous. As it stands, it's still going to take Sandy until late-afternoon to arrive at the family cabin past Dechambault Lake. A trip she's been looking forward to for weeks. That's why she's diligent and made sure she packed everything she might need last night before going to bed. She made sure to check the forecast too, which promised clear and cold this morning. Inaccuracy. It's what perturbs her now. Any variation in road conditions could spell trouble. Especially travelling north. But she is determined even if snow falls or there is a shift in the wind that there will be no change in plans. Uncle says he'll have a big pot of fish chowder ready. She can't pass up that.

Almost ready to go except for Misty. "Come on girl. In you go. That's a good dog. Pretty soon you will meet everyone in our family." Misty is a mongrel. With her short, vanilla-coloured hair, Sandy figures she might have some pit bull in her blood. As always, the dog is happy to go for a ride, wagging her tail before hurriedly jumping onto the passenger seat.

Sandy hadn't planned on getting a dog just yet. Figured maybe she'd wait a few years until she purchased a condo with a fenced yard. But Misty stole her heart the moment they met. Having just moved into a rented, beautiful, old two-storey home in Regina's Cathedral Village neighbourhood, Sandy had been puttering around in her small kitchen unpacking the night Misty had arrived. When she took some empty boxes to the alley for recycling, the dog was rooting around in a garbage can that had been knocked on its side. She had no collar and no tag and she followed Sandy in to her new home as though she owned the place. Sandy placed ads in a community newsletter and with the local SPCA, but nothing turned up. No one claimed Misty, who was named because of weather conditions the night Sandy found her in the alley. They've been together almost a year now. Today would be Misty's first substantial road trip.

It is a special homecoming. Valentine's weekend and Sandy has promised her sister Charlene that she'll bring an ice cream cake from Dairy Queen. Can't find one of those in Descham-bault. And, it is an easy promise to keep. With temperatures hovering between minus twenty-five and minus thirty outside, it is impossible that the cake will melt. She's double-wrapped it in Indian suitcases, as Charlene would say. Two heavy garbage bags to keep the freshness in. It makes Sandy smile.

Besides, great friends can always be counted on. Sandy had her best friend, Kyle, rig up a carrying case on the back door of her Jeep, specifically for the cake. Strapped into the same place where her bike is usually carried during summer months.

Long road trip or not, the destination is all Sandy's thought about for days. "Going home." She says it out loud for God to hear. Immediately, she is forced to wipe away a tear of gratitude that threatens to obscure her vision. All the while, she still glances at the new mirror ornament that Joe gave her.

Joe Bush Sr. stopped by while she was packing up. By chance, he had been visiting the Queen City to speak at a police commissioners meeting, offering suggestions on how to improve relations between Regina's Native population and the police. One of his ideas is being met with such enthusiasm. That is, to get out of the main police building and set up satellite offices within high schools and community centres. Sandy has a good feeling the plan might come about soon. So does Joe.

Joe gave Sandy a warm hug and said, "You need to connect with your roots, Sandy, your family. This trip is good." He gave her a round piece of braided sweetgrass, wrapped in a red cloth, to hang from her mirror. "Because red is the only colour that attracts the spirits. This'll keep you safe on the road," he says. "They will guide you." Interestingly enough, red has always been Sandy's favourite colour. Now she knows why. It makes her happy to see the braid hanging from her rearview mirror.

Sandy knows the braid of sweetgrass will offer her even more reassurance than the Saint Christopher medal she's had dangling from her rearview. Ever since she bought her first Jeep, five years ago. "Saint Christopher is the Patron Saint for travellers," Sandy's Baba had told her. "It'll keep you safe each time you come home to visit." Baba has passed now. Sandy misses her every single day. Sandy was adopted and she knows the strong bond between them was forged in the heart and not through biology. That is why Saint Christopher remains in the Jeep and hangs alongside the braid. Two faiths travelling in unison.

Three hours go by quickly and despite the cold and some drifting, the road conditions are good. Sandy notices traffic is light for a weekend morning, as she makes her way through the city of Prince Albert. It tickles her to see the KFC enroute. Sandy remembers a joke Charlene told her. "People seem to think the north begins in La Ronge. But it really starts in P.A. That's where the last KFC is!" Sandy stops in and picks up a bucket of chicken.

She so looks forward to seeing her sister again. And she wonders if the rest of her biological family is just as giddy with excitement about this weekend gathering. She hopes so. She has been dreaming of this visit ever since she can remember.

3. PREMONITION

TRAVELLING ALONE ON NORTHERN HIGHWAYS can be both exhilarating and frightening. The pavement is like an unwelcome visitor breaking up the pristine wilderness that kisses the skyline. As Sandy passes by massive rock formations which dot the Precambrian landscape, she feels as though each large stone is telling her a story. Beckoning her to continue further into the wild.

The Grandfathers.

It's how an Elder might refer to each grand mass of rock.

There aren't a lot of rest stops along this highway, nor many rest stops along any northern stretch of roadway. But there is a place called Bloomfields that is half way between Prince Albert and Deschambault Lake. Sandy expects it'll resemble a rustic log cabin structure that blends in with the landscape. She can't know for sure, having only heard about it from Charlene and now seeing it as a dot on a map. But, it is a necessary break for her and will allow her a chance to stretch her legs, fill up the gas tank, visit the bathroom, and pick up a sandwich and another coffee.

The forecasted snow has turned out to be a few large flakes that dance and glisten as they fall. Sandy is grateful for good road conditions and the flawed weather forecasting. She's passed only two vehicles in the last hundred kilometres. If anything happened, she'd find herself alone and stranded with the silence of the land.

She estimates another ten minutes before her planned stop. Good timing. Sandy knows enough to fill up her gas tank anywhere gas is available while driving in the north. You never know how far it is to the next gas station. Could spell disaster. Plus, she is in need of facilities. Misty is wiggling around and starting to pant. A dog's language that she also needs to pee.

Sandy decides to take care of Misty first, and pulls up alongside a picturesque bridge in the wilderness. She is practising her Cree and struggles to remember the pronunciation of the small river—Puskwakau.

Even though the water should be frozen in gleeful rest of the winter season, Sandy can hear trickling and she sees small torrents of running water sneaking through what is mostly ice on the river bed. The air is fresh and Sandy exhilarates in the feeling of its clean coldness caressing her face. It feels like heaven. There is no sound other than a gentle wind rustling the snow-covered branches of jackpine. No smell other than peace.

It is the reason Sandy is startled. Misty, meanwhile, pays no attention to apparent dangers of the forest. The pup is just content to be outdoors and free, sniffling along the shoreline. But Sandy hears something in the bush and starts to worry about wildlife. She knows bears hibernate and this is bear country. But cougars do not hibernate nor migrate in winter. She wants to pull little Misty closer, but she didn't use a leash. She let the dog run free. Sandy starts to panic. Whatever is watching her from the bush is getting closer. She can feel a change in energy.

Sandy yells, "Come on, Misty! Time to go." She makes a whistling sound with her lips that the dog usually responds to. But Misty seems unaware of any danger and is oblivious. Instead of responding, Misty runs further into the bush. Then the dog disappears into a labyrinth of brush covered in snow. Sandy is horrified and time stands still.

She still doesn't know if what happened next is real, or is a figment of her of over-stressed imagination, brought on because of the long drive or a lack of sleep.

Sandy hears Misty emit a bark. Not the sound of pain, but the way her dog responds when she's happy to see someone familiar. Sandy watches as snow softly falls from untouched branches. The places where people do not tread in winter. Then she wonders, do my ears betray me? Sandy hears the soft murmur of laughter coming from the underbrush where Misty disappeared.

She is paralyzed at what emerges from the clearing. There is no room for her to retreat. A small trickle of urine escapes her bladder and Sandy holds her breath in anticipation of the unknown. What she sees is not a wolf. Not a cougar. Not a man. But a Centaur—half-man and half what appears to be the bold body of an elk. The brute carries Misty back to the safety of the snow-covered shoreline. He seems as tall as the trees; deeply muscled and donning an enormous set of antlers. The Centaur gently places the dog on the ground, points his finger towards Sandy and smiles. The Centaur then disappears like a mist. Sandy is still—too afraid to move.

Was this real? Did it really happen? Am I hallucinating? What the hell?

Misty returns to where Sandy is standing—near the Jeep—like nothing out of the ordinary has just happened. The dog's had her pee and stretched her legs and is happy to get back into the Jeep. Sandy shakes her head and squints to see if remnants of what she thought she just saw might remain. But there is nothing but silence and beauty and snow. In the meantime, Misty barks happily: it's time to go. Sandy opens the passenger door and lets the pup jump in.

It is a short distance to the gas station where she'd planned to stop. But her mind won't stop. Again she asks herself, *What just happened?*

Her hands tremble on the steering wheel, but she's not about to stop a second time. She is fully unnerved and is still shaking in disbelief. Who knows what else will come out of the woods?

Sandy thinks about a recent story she prepared for the newsroom. It was a feature about a tattoo competition. The winning artist had fashioned a Centaur across the blank canvas of the back of a twenty-year-old woman. She remembers the artist's explanation of why the image of the Centaur was chosen.

Centaurs are a paradox. They signify higher learning and exploration, and conflict between primal nature and civilized culture. The bow is female symbol, while the arrow is male symbol. The Centaur suggests the need to find human balance.

It makes Sandy curious. Why did this Centaur show himself to her? If she even really saw a Centaur.

4. DESCHAMBAULT

LISTENING INTENTLY TO THE MELODIC VOICE of Uncle Gabriel, Sandy finds herself holding her breath, anticipating where the story he's telling might go next. It's a perfect setting. A small cabin in the isolated woods. Snow is falling and the moonlight streams in through the large picture window. All is hushed except for the quiet cadence of the Old Man's voice.

"Deschambault. It's what everyone calls the lake now. But Mooshum, that's Cree for Grandfather, Mooshum referred to what happened as wapawikoscikanik. Translated from Cree, it suggests there is danger, and it means 'The Narrows of Fear.'"

"This is how the story goes," Uncle Gabriel settles in and continues. "There was a slaughter near Pelican Narrows, just before reaching the lake at Deschambault. It happened in 1729 according to Hudson Bay journals." He talks non-stop for the next twenty minutes, The story is so fascinating it feels more like twenty seconds, as he methodically recounts the details.

A group of Sioux canoed down the South Saskatchewan River—making their way up north—through Deschambault Lake. Their plan was to raid a Cree village near Opawikoscikan. Pelican Narrows. The Sioux waited until most of the Cree men had left on a hunting trip. This story was handed down because some of the Cree villagers survived that raid. They knew the Sioux were coming. A Cree gifted with medicine had had a vision and was able to convince some of the residents to leave before the Sioux arrived. Only a handful listened, those who believed in medicine and visions, and knew what the medicine man had seen was real. And it was those who fled who watched in horror as the massacre unfolded.

They witnessed beheadings at the point of sharp hunting knives that were swung like bayonets. Bloody arrows protruding from the last gasps of breath as old women fell to the ground, pierced through the throat. The sickening sounds of the bludgeoning of scalps of children. Their lifeless bodies left to twitch as brain matter seeped from their open skulls.

Wapawikoscikanik. The Narrows of Fear.

The Sioux left, taking what they could, including the young women. They thought themselves victors. They were wrong.

When the Cree hunters returned later that same day, they found the dead bodies of their loved ones. Those who had survived told the men where the Sioux were headed. A war party was quickly assembled. Because the Cree knew the land and the waterways, they were able to take a short cut. That war party waited in ambush at Opawikoscikanik. All but one of the Sioux were killed. The Cree let one Sioux survive so he could retell the story.

"Don't mess with the Northern Cree!" Uncle Gabriel lets out a howl delivering that last line and he takes a bite of bannock. Sandy figures he's told and retold this story a hundred times. "Here have some more fish chowder my girl. You're too skinny." He is finishing up his second piece of KFC chicken. A drumstick.

Sandy covers the empty bowl in front of her with her hand, feeling guilty for doing so. But she has totally lost her appetite. The story is so graphic, violent and unsettling. She knows it is cultural protocol to accept when someone offers more food, but she simply can't. Holy. Over this past hour, she's already eaten more in one sitting than she usually does over an entire weekend. And what a feast. Fry bread and baked bannock with raisins. Rice pudding and berries. Hearty homestyle fish chowder—catch of the day. Moose meat with neckbones and potatoes. And the KFC. Sandy feels the need to loosen the belt on her pants.

Or "pantses" as her sister Charlene says. When Sandy walked through the door earlier in the evening, Charlene had squealed, "I love your outfit. Where did you get those pantses?" It had made Sandy laugh. And, she's now made a mental note to buy her sister a pair of harem pants— comfortably loose and baggy Genie pants—as Sandy likes to think of them—that are only found in fashion outlets in the larger cities.

Sandy is still smiling and basking in the warmth of a steady wood stove in the cabin, listening with fascination to stories that are her own family history.

"Well, if you won't have any more to eat then maybe Misty will." With wrinkled hands, the Old Man rips some moose meat from a bone and gives it to the happy pup, who is sitting beside his wooden chair. "We don't usually let dogs in the house, you know. But this one is an exception. Kind of like you Sandy. Given leeway to break with knowledge, traditions or protocol because you haven't yet learned. It's okay." Gabriel reassures. "It's so good to sit with you."

He makes eye contact with Charlene and points with his chin towards another part of the house. Without saying a word, he's urging Charlene to bring him the photo albums. And even though Charlene is mid-neckbone and with greasy fingers, she knows her cue. She lays what's left of her seventh neckbone on her dinner plate, smiles at Sandy, and heads to another room at the end of the hall.

There is comfortable silence as Gabriel continues to fuss over Misty. Maynard, Uncle Gabriel's son, seems to be off in some other place, poking at his now cold boiled potatoes. It seems obvious that he's thinking of something that has nothing to do with enjoying an evening of meeting his cousin for the first time. Sandy silently admits that the only thing that would make this visit even better would have been if her younger brother Larry was able to be here this weekend as well.

"But that crazy bugger is off on his own adventures. Climbing up a mountain. Imagine that," Uncle Gabriel snorts. It's then Sandy learns that Larry has always had a dream to conquer Mount Kilimanjaro in the African country of Tanzania.

"He's got a six-month adventure planned," Maynard muses. "It was on his bucket list. Next he's off to the Serengeti in the northern part of that country. He'll be gone for more than a year."

"Well, I can hardly wait to hear his stories when he returns," Sandy says, and takes a leisurely sip of tea. She has finally stopped fidgeting from the disturbing graphic stories of Sioux warrior attacks.

She uses these moments to glance around the cabin.

It was such a warm and wonderful greeting when she first arrived: hugs, smiles, and the smell of good food cooking. The cabin is made of logs. Built by Gabriel himself. Each log chosen for its sturdiness. Each plank shaved with love.

Gabriel's wife, Auntie Myrna, died a year ago. Sandy is sad that she never met her Auntie, having heard so many good stories about her from Charlene, in the many telephone conversations they've had these past several months, since meeting. Char said that Uncle Gabriel was lost in grief after Auntie's death. He'd stopped talking for an entire month and he'd sat by the wood stove day and night. That's why Maynard decided to stay home after the funeral, instead of returning to his job in Prince Albert.

Sandy wishes she had been able to go to the funeral. But she wasn't able to get the time off at work. Two employees were on maternity leave and the newsroom was short-staffed. Besides, Sandy didn't want her first official family visit to be shrouded in sadness. She sent a lovely wreath instead, along with her regrets.

Maynard is an only child, which is rare in Aboriginal families. But the couple always considered him a blessing, and that Myrna was able to conceive at all. Repeated rapes when she went to residential school meant that Myrna suffered from venereal disease, which almost robbed her of her fertility entirely. Charlene is a good source of health information like this about her family. It's why Sandy now knows to be mindful of diet. Diabetes, something Sandy hopes to avoid. The Old Man suffers from it.

As Sandy continues looking around the cabin, she wonders why this family of avid fishers have no stuffed and mounted trophies of catches on the walls. What Sandy sees instead is a wall of proud history. Framed black-and-white photos of ancestors with the strength to change the world. Sandy sits at a hand-made wooden table, in view of a pot rack that hangs just above a butcher's block. No doubt many moose, elk, and deer have been processed and wrapped right here. The cupboards have no doors, exposing a medley of memories. Some contain fine china. Others have mason jars that are sometimes used as drinking glasses, and at other times used for canning. Some hold old mugs stained with endless conversations over tea and honey.

The family room holds the warmth that emanates from a cast iron wood stove. There are four comfortable chairs around the stove. No television. There is no need to travel within the imagination of anyone else. The large picture window reveals a paradise—a pristine northern landscape.

Sandy feels blessed to be sitting here in this cabin with her newly-discovered family.

5. FISHING SHACK ATTACK

THIS TIME OF YEAR THE MORNING SUN doesn't fully rise until after nine a.m. in this part of the north. But Uncle Gabriel has been up for hours—packing last night's leftovers—some KFC—and brewing coffee in an old percolator. He knows that Sandy has never gone ice fishing before and he is eager to share the experience. But he will not wake her. Instead, he makes his way to Maynard's bedroom to rouse him to get ready for their day.

Gabriel glances at the pencil marks that have charted his son's growth over many years. Maynard's progress from a boy to a man celebrated on the doorframe that leads to his bedroom. Gabriel doesn't knock. He pushes the hardwood door open and intends to gently touch the shoulders of his son to wake him. But for a moment the Old Man is taken aback. There are remnants of lipstick on Maynard's face. Puzzled, Gabriel rationalizes that he must have kissed his cousin Sandy good night before going to bed. It looks like the same colour that was on her lips when she first arrived. Yes, that must be the reason.

"My boy. Miyo wapanisi. Time to get up. We're taking Sandy fishing soon. You have to load the sled."

"Oh, okay. What about the dog?" Maynard yawns and wipes the sleep from his eyes.

"Misty is staying home with Charlene, who will be making us some moose stew today. Misty will like that. Being able to eat the gristle. Besides, the shack is too small. Come. I made some coffee."

Sandy hears them and before long she has joined them in the kitchen.

Within the hour, the three are standing in warm sunlight on a cold, frozen lake. Uncle Gabriel is unlocking the fishing shack. "Good thing we'll be mostly inside today, Sandy," Maynard smirks. "Can't say you are properly dressed. I packed an extra pair of ski pants for you, just in case. But don't fart in them because farts have no way to escape in ski pants. They are air tight." Maynard winks at her and adds, "Love your Fluevog boots."

Sandy giggles and checks her boots. They are a deep fuchsia colour and are tightly-fitted with decorative lacing. When Sandy bought them she had figured they would go with any outfit. But she wonders how Maynard knows this designer.

It takes no time at all for the wood stove to be lit, the honey holes to be re-opened with a small hatchet, and the tea to be boiling—even though there is a thermos filled with coffee. "Wihkaskwapoy. Wild spearmint," The Old Man tells her as he hands Sandy a metal cup. "We harvest it every fall. Lots of mint grows just down the road from my home. You take some leaves when you head back to the city." The fragrant brew reminds Sandy of her childhood and her love of chewing peppermints.

Sandy fondly recollects that it is Baba whose memory she's always associated with the flavour of mint. Baba would give them to Sandy as a treat when she was a little girl. Now a grown woman she will have another fond memory of mint. And those memories are in the making, smiling back at her as she sips. She is touched and feels a soft lump forming in her throat. She decides to offer a silent prayer of gratitude to the spirits for guiding her here today, and bringing the cup up to her nose, she inhales the sweet smell of wihkaskwapoy to remember this moment.

"I cannot get over how much you remind me of your mother, Sandy. She used to sniff her food and tea before putting it in her body. In fact, just sitting here with you reminds me of when we all were kids. Your mom loved ice fishing. She loved being outdoors period." Uncle Gabriel wipes away a tear from the corner of his eye. But before he is able to continue, they hear the sound of footsteps outside on the ice.

It causes Maynard to tense. "Hey Dad, maybe it's that sandwich salesman again." He snickers.

The Old Man laughs too, adding, "Well, I didn't bring any money today and I packed up some food. So if it's him, he's out of luck."

Maynard secretly has hopes that it might be the young stranger again.

As for Sandy's thoughts? In some irrational recess of her mind, she worries that it might be the Centaur.

There is no knock. The door swings open abruptly, letting in a cold blast of arctic air.

6. THE PROCLAIMER

"**H**EY. IT'S JOHN WAYNE." Maynard gets up from his small fishing stool to give the visitor a hug. "Hey, it's good to see you my friend."

Uncle Gabriel greets the man with a smile. "Sandy, this is your cousin. John Wayne." She giggles upon hearing the name. "Seriously?"

The big man immediately invades her personal space, hugging her too tightly, which makes her grimace. Sandy can smell that he's just had some coffee and that he likely smudged this morning. The residual scent of sweetgrass is familiar to her and brings her some comfort. She associates the scent with Joe Bush Sr., the first Elder Sandy met months ago, and the reason she decided to dig even deeper into her own past. The reason she is sitting here with family right now.

Sandy's newly-introduced cousin studies her face, "Oh my Lord. You look just like your mom. So wonderful to meet you. And, yes, my first name is John and my middle name is Wayne. But I'm no Indian fighter. Cha! I fight for the Indians." John sticks out his tongue as he laughs at his own joke. "Hey, I brought this for you. Carved it myself." From the pocket of his racing-green-coloured Canada Goose parka, John produces a delicate carving in the shape of a bear. "It's part of an elk horn. Spirits told me you should have it."

Sandy examines the intricate design, wondering, "How could this new cousin possibly know about my dreams of bears? We've only just met." She is no expert on carving but as Sandy holds the little bear in her palm, she thinks, "This feels more like some type of manmade material rather than bone." Thoughts aside, she graciously thanks him. "Maskosis. Kinanaskomitin." A little bear, thank you. Her pronunciation is off.

John smiles, appreciating her effort to speak Cree. From that moment on, John Wayne takes over the conversation. His boundaries include no small talk.

"Hey, wihkaskwapoy." John points with his lips towards the mint tea. Without being asked to do so, Maynard pours him a cup. An old dance that's been played for years. As the mug is being passed, Sandy notices that John wears bulky silver and turquoise rings on each of his hands. "Mint tea. Good for the digestive system." John holds his mug in the air offering cheers to Sandy, then he immediately wanders into territory that should be off-limits when meeting someone new and for the first time.

"So, you drink, Sandy?"

"You mean alcohol?"

"Yes. The bad stuff." John Wayne carefully analyzes her response as he continues to sip wihkaskwapoy.

"Not anymore. I used to drink wine, but I found it interferes with my creativity. And you?" Sandy cannot figure out why she offered up an answer. It's none of his business. Where's he going with this?

It's like John Wayne knows her thoughts.

"Good for you sister. Women are sacred and deserve to be protected and respected. That respect starts with self. I used to drink as well. All of us did at one point. Being lost is the reason. That damn Catholic church and residential school tried to kill our people."

At this statement, Uncle Gabriel holds his mug in the air, reciting the words, "Hiy hiy."

John continues. "It's why I built a sweat lodge. Learned the teachings from some people in Manitoba. Our own spirituality is helping to heal so many of our people, Sandy. You ever been to a ceremony?"

Again, Sandy thinks, too personal of a query. But she feels compelled to answer anyway, as though she has something to prove. "Yes. Down south. I've been traditionally adopted by an Elder named Joe. Met him by chance. He's taught me a lot."

"There is no such thing as chance." John reaches into his parka pocket again, this time pulling out a small pouch made from blue broadcloth. "Do you know what this is?"

Sandy hesitates. "Well. My guess is it might be some type of medicine."

"Bingo." John takes Sandy's hand and places the pouch in her palm, "I brought this for you. The colour blue represents new beginnings. You belong here in Deschambault with your family. It's good you came. I am holding a ceremony tonight. Will you be able to come?"

As much as John seems to be studying Sandy's reactions, she is also examining him. The chiselled jaw line. His protruding nose, which has sustained some permanent damage, likely caused by excessive use of alcohol in his past. John's salt and pepper hair pulled back in a tight braid. Sandy can't place him, but there is something familiar about him, like she's seen him before. Somewhere. She offers an answer, "Certainly I can go, unless Uncle Gabriel has other plans." The Old Man shakes his head, indicating no.

"You keep this pouch and pray with it every morning at sunrise. It is sage. I picked it myself last July. A sacred rite for only a few. Not just anyone is allowed to pick medicines. I've been taught that it is forbidden unless you are pure."

Sandy doesn't say anything but she thinks there is something wrong with his statement.

John's declaration reminds her of a time not that long ago.

Because she grew up as an adopted child and lived in a white community, away from her own Native culture, someone once forbade her from dancing at pow wows. They'd said, "Because you didn't grow up in our culture, you will never know how to show the proper respect. So you are not allowed to dance." It broke Sandy's heart. She so longed to celebrate and move to the beat of the drum but, as a result of those words, she denied herself the opportunity. That is until she met Old Joe Bush, Sr., an Elder and spiritual leader. He told her anyone can dance. Anyone can celebrate our culture.

So, sitting here now, Sandy is pretty sure John's thinking is askew about picking sage. She makes a mental note to ask Joe next time she sees him. But mostly, Sandy wonders why John Wayne would make that kind of exclusionary pronouncement to her—that only certain people are "allowed" to pick sage?

Does he think I am unpure? She wishes she had the courage to ask this out loud. But Sandy doesn't want to offend. She's just met these members of her biological family. She remains silent, and guesses that John Wayne has no problem being intrusive and offensive. She makes another mental note to be cautious any time he's around.

7. GABRIEL

THE OLD MAN NEVER ADMITS IT, but he's tired again this morning. Bad sleep. For years, he's tried almost everything he can think of to have a restful sleep: chamomile tea, boiled rat root tea, soaking in a hot bathtub. Sometimes these things make Gabriel sleepy but he's never found anything that totally erases the stains on his memory. The ones that surface at night, always messing with peaceful slumber. Too often, and when he is unable to push the images away. They just come. Always haunting.

Gabriel is eleven. He and dorm-mate Billy are no longer boys. Not yet men. They are at that in-between stage where questions are more prevalent than answers. They are still required to attend the residential school. Still feeling like prisoners, but over these years they have figured out how to fit in without the constant worry of physical punishment.

Gabriel and Billy have been assigned to kitchen duty: peeling carrots and potatoes, washing pots, sweeping the floor. It's a sad, forced routine that the boys try to lighten when none of the Brothers are near enough to see or hear them. Sometimes the boys even laugh out loud, as though genuinely happy. A difficult feat in a place like this.

It's a Wednesday. Young Gabriel knows this because there are pieces of canned meat stewing—akin to Spam—with tomatoes and onions for tonight's supper. The same as every

Wednesday. The potatoes he peels will be added along with the smallest bit of salt. There is only one window in this cold steel kitchen and it's too high up to see anything but the tops of trees. But from his point of view, Gabriel can tell that it is windy outside and the sky is overcast.

Gabriel studies the potato he holds in his hand. It has several eyes and two roots protruding. He remembers a story told by his Kohkum, his Grandmother. The roots will tell you how many loves you will have in your life. Love? Is this what he feels when Billy pokes him in the ribs with that carrot he's holding? Gabriel giggles and the boys chase each other around the heavy wooden butcher's block in the middle of the industrial kitchen. Will they get caught? Brother Thorn has a case of diarrhea and spends more time in the lavatory today than keeping tabs on his charge. So the boys are free to express right now.

Billy tackles Gabriel.

They fall together.

Gabriel always wakes in a panicked sweat. His nightly ordeal is accompanied by a sense of bewilderment and guilt. What happened to Billy? One day, he just disappeared.

Hiding for safety at the back of his consciousness, Gabriel knows. He's heard the stories. And he heard the muffled cries. Billy was his dorm-mate. Slept in the cot beside him.

A year later. It is early winter. A twelve-year-old Gabriel pretends to be asleep upon hearing the footsteps in the night. Sock-footed but audible. The raspy breath of Brother Thorn, "Come with me." Then the sound of two sets of footprints disappearing into cavernous darkness.

Billy is never seen again and no one says a word.

But the smell of burned flesh and sin hangs over the incinerator room as a sick shadow for weeks. No one asks questions. Nothing is explained. Billy's shoes, clothes, and school books are just quickly removed. No one ever tells Billy's parents that he's disappeared. Brother Thorn is sent to another residential school.

Gabriel cries only once about Billy ceasing to exist, vanishing without a trace. And his sobs come only when no one is watching. Always. No witness.

8. MAYNARD

MAYNARD HAS ALWAYS BEEN SPECIAL and different from everyone around him. As a seven-year-old boy, Maynard was skinny, like a twig. Even though he ate like a lumberjack. His hair was always unkempt. His nose always snotty. No one cared because he always did his chores.

It was a rare occasion that Auntie Myrna and Uncle Gabriel needed a babysitter for young Maynard. They usually would take him with them—which wasn't surprising because most of their family trips meant going out on the land to pick berries, cut wood, set snares, or go fishing.

This trip was different. Maybe the couple considered it a date night? So they left their young son behind. There was celebration to be had.

It was because Uncle Gabriel held a new record for catching the biggest fish in Saskatchewan. A twelve-pound white fish right here in Deschambault Lake. He even got his picture in the local newspaper holding the monster, which was large enough to feed twenty people. They know that for sure because that's how many people showed up at the impromptu community feast—in Auntie Myrna's kitchen—once they all heard about the catch. It was the talk of the town for years.

And for this special evening, the talk of an industry. An Outdoor Sports Awards ceremony and gala dinner was honouring Uncle Gabriel in Prince Albert. It was going to be an overnight trip, but no doubt Auntie Myrna would make Uncle take her to the Thrift Store before heading back up north.

Maynard would be looked after by cousin Charlene. She was a teen then, but only a bit taller than her young cousin. The two were as close as siblings.

Cousins. They had a nice night together. Talking, laughing, joking.

Charlene was your typical teenage girl in many ways. She was blossoming, and doing stuff like plucking her eyebrows and shaving her legs. "I even found some type of wax in the store the other day, Maynard."

"You making candles?"

"No, silly head. They're called waxing strips. I was reading the back of the box and it says using this will make my legs silky smooth. Better than shaving they say."

"Did the wax work?" Little Maynard seems genuinely interested.

"Not really. The strips were so small. They hardly pulled off any hair before the wax got all hard again and I couldn't use it. And it hurt. Left a red mark." Charlene pulls up the bottom of her jeans to show him. "But what bothers me the most is that I paid five dollars for it."

"Holy!" Maynard exclaims. "You should have just gone to the hardware and bought some duct tape!" He laughs and snorts at the same time, "It would have cost only seventy-five cents and probably done a better job." Howls from them both at that one.

"Hungry?" Charlene asks.

"A bit," he says.

Auntie Myrna has left some moose meat to fry and some potatoes to boil. So they start to fry. Little Maynard grabs a bottle of ketchup from the ice box.

Later, they play checkers and then they play fish with a deck of cards. Not a worry in the world. Charlene feels like a grown up being left in charge. But in case of any concerns, there were always other relatives nearby if need be. Their phone numbers were written on a piece of paper that had been taped to the fridge.

Charlene would be getting a whole ten dollars for babysitting! It was a lot of money back then. With the other money she has saved, it meant she could finally go to the Northern Store to buy those new jeans she'd been eyeing and a new tube of lipstick too. And sweet and salty snacks of course.

Once the sun started to go down and the tops of trees outside the big window were barely visible, Charlene decided it was time to get Maynard ready for bed. She made sure he brushed his little strong teeth, which were so often chewing on dry meat. As he brushed, Charlene smacked on her current favourite lip colour as she looked in the mirror. It was a fiery red and almost empty. She left it on the bathroom counter, and shooed the boy off to be tucked in. A new Nancy Drew book was waiting once it was quiet in the cabin.

Charlene awoke next morning. Nancy Drew was on the floor but Charlene was still on the couch. It was where she fell asleep and where she was woken up by someone rattling around in the kitchen. Little Maynard was fixing himself some cereal.

But there was something different about him that morning.

He was wearing her lip colour.

9. JOHN WAYNE

"IT WAS A FEW SUMMERS AGO when this happened, but it's something which never should have happened at all." Charlene shares with her sister a tale almost too unbelievable to be true. "I'm not even a pow wow dancer and even I know that how my cousin acted was out of line."

Char says that she's never been impressed by what she calls John Wayne's phony baloney: "That he's so spiritually-gifted. But it is how he presents himself, which means he ought to know that a pow wow is a celebration of culture, community, and an expression of that love through dance and song."

It's true—the drum moves the spirit. And most people know full-well that a pow wow shouldn't be regarded the same as a spiritual ceremony, like a sweat lodge.

"It's why I can't figure out what made him act like an ass the last time he went to Beardy's. Glad I wasn't there for this. How embarrassing." Beardy's and Okemasis Cree Nation is an Aboriginal community not far from Prince Albert.

"As the story goes, everyone was having a great time at this gathering. Until John Wayne decided to ruin it. Someday, he will have to face up to it. I wonder if I will be there when that day comes." Charlene continues to reiterate what she's heard about this shameful day.

The movement at any pow wow was constant. Prairie grasses swayed. Children ran around in brightly-coloured outfits. Statuesque Old Women covered in hand-beaded shawls spoke wisdom without saying a word. The coffee and laughter were aplenty.

The only real negative about any pow wow are the porta potties. Necessary, basic, but offering no real privacy.

John had set up his tipi close to the pow wow arbour where everyone gathers to dance. It was maybe a half hour before they would begin to assemble for Grand Entry, where hundreds of dancers move as one. The Grand Entry signals the start of the pow wow.

He figured he best not wait till the last minute to take care of some business. There were no lineups at a blue fibreglass toilet about twenty metres away from where John was standing. He headed toward it.

Holy. Whoever was in there was taking a long time.

It was obviously a dancer. John heard the sound of jingle cones tinkling together and the sound of someone pulling toilet paper from the roll. He wished she'd hurry up already. The noon day sun was making beads of sweat trickle down his forehead. Or maybe he was all jittery because a big bowel movement beckoned and he's needing to eject. Soon.

He thought to himself that it would be weird to knock on the door. Knocking might scare her into staying inside this little house on the prairie longer than even she'd like. The smell was no reason to stay in there. Only business. John was forced to wait.

He heard her pulling toilet paper from the roll again and wondered again why girls always took so long?

Finally, the door nudged open and a teenage jingle dress dancer emerged, dressed in shiny red satin. She averted her eyes when she passed him.

John grabbed the door before it had a chance to close. In a millisecond he rushed in. Couldn't wait another moment. Next were sound effects. One big fart followed by the sounds of hallelujahs. But when he was done, John did something unusual. He looked down the shit hole and was outraged by what he saw. Yes, poop, lots of it. And a used bloody tampon.

Incensed, he flung open the toilet door to bright sunlight. He wanted to see where that young dancer had gone. He didn't wash his hands in the portable washing stall outside. Instead, when he noticed a flash of her red satin near the tipi set up beside his own. John hastened over to where the young teenager was standing.

But only for a moment. He stopped abruptly. Because in that moment, a thought occurred to him: "She needs to be taught a lesson and I'm gonna be the one to teach her."

John glanced around. There was always security nearby at any pow wow. When he spotted the brightly yellow construction vest that the security guards wear, he ran in that direction.

"These people need to be evicted. Removed from the premises," John bellowed at the young guard, pointing at the tipi erected next to his—the place where he saw the dancer with the red dress putting on her feathers.

The security guard seemed bewildered. So he asked John for more details. The two walked to the security kiosk and, once there, John also shared his indignation with the director of security. "I don't know who those people are who set up camp next to mine. But they shouldn't be here. The girl is on her moon time."

"How do you know this?" the head of security had to ask.

"Because she took her sweet time in the john. When she came out, she was acting kind of guilty. When I went in, I noticed a bloody tampon down the chute."

"I will see what I can do." The security director seemed flustered.

John waited and paced.

But the security director did nothing. John knew this for sure because moments later, at Grand Entry, he saw the young girl's red satin dress in amongst the other dancers. And no one was moving flaps and poles at the tipi next to his. He was certain that red dress dancer was camping there with her family.

This was scandalous in his mind. On her moon time and coming to the pow wow anyway. Security was taking too long. So he went to the announcer's booth to complain to the pow wow committee. He actually convinced a couple of male committee members to come with him to take a look down the shit hole for themselves.

Yes, there was a tampon. But how can anyone prove the young jingle dress dancer was the one who put it there?

"Maybe we should ask her family?"

"Yes maybe," a committee member suggests.

John Wayne's fury increased. "Ask? Ask? There is the evidence right there!" He pointed at the tampon and he ordered security to tell the family to leave. Ordered them.

The uproar caused such a stink that the family was eventually told they were not welcome to stay.

Never once is a woman named Nina Thomas consulted. She was the Head Woman Dancer at that pow wow and she may very well have handled this situation differently. As for the young jingle dress dancer, well, she wasn't on her time. But no one asked.

"How do you know all of this stuff?" Sandy is appalled by what she's just been told, remembering only too well those who have tried to stop her from learning and calling it tradition that they allow themselves to interfere. It causes damage and can only be seen as lateral violence.

"Well, we have the same last name John Wayne and me. That's how I found out. Moccasin Telegraph. People talk and, really, our community is not that large." Charlene then quickly changes the subject. Sandy has noticed that Charlene often switches topics if the discussion turns unpleasant. Actually, everyone in the family seems to do that. "But let's not talk about that. Look," Charlene points out the large picture window, "how beautiful it is today. I say we take Misty for another walk."

10. INSIGHTS

WHAT GOOD IS INTIMACY when in theory only? A cold morning at the fishing shack, despite the wood stove. Good tea and good company, but Sandy received no real insight into her past from Uncle Gabriel. It is what Sandy hopes to find during this visit.

Again she asked pointed questions about her mom. Her mom's personality? Her likes and dislikes. Her quirks and habits. Uncle Gabriel smiled, but didn't offer much. Why?

Sandy can only guess that maybe it's simply a guy thing to not delve too deeply into matters of the heart. Maybe it makes Uncle Gabriel uncomfortable. Or maybe it unearths other memories, which are not pleasant? Sandy hopes to have more luck with Charlene.

She's no longer sitting in the ice shack with the guys. The afternoon is warm and she is sitting at the kitchen table, sipping another tea and peeling potatoes with her sister. Another stew is on the menu. The meat has been cooking slowly all day so it will be tender. The spuds are a hearty side dish.

"You coming to John Wayne's sweat tonight?" Sandy is hoping that she will not be the only woman there. That is, if she even chooses to go. Charlene's pow wow story makes Sandy think she may not want to get to know her cousin at all. Even if he is family.

"Nah. Never got into that even though old John makes it sound like we'll all go to hell if we don't attend. Kind of like what the church says if you don't follow their beliefs. Besides," and Charlene lowers her voice, "I didn't even like him when we were kids. Why would I go out of my way to hang out with him now?"

"Why's that."

"We've already talked about Beardy's, which makes me think he is a perfect example of everything that's wrong in this world. He goes to that sweat lodge, I think, just for his public appearance. So others will think he's spiritual. Like being there will absolve and cancel out everything he's done. But he never tells them the truth about himself, only what he thinks others want to hear—people who don't know him well." She pauses, then adds, "Besides, he used to hurt me."

Charlene changes the subject again, "You've never had moose stew before? Neckbones, yes. But you are in for a treat for to-night's supper." Moving away from an uncomfortable subject and from the kitchen table, Charlene gives Sandy a quick smile and walks towards one of the cupboards. She removes an old pot, which has seen better days, and starts to fill it with water. Sandy knows enough to stop her questioning, "This enough potatoes or do you think I should peel some more?" Again small talk softens the moment, and Sandy is confused about the insistence on keeping the conversation light.

"Oh, more is always better. We fry the leftover with onions in the morning. Really good with eggs and toast."

11. NO SHOW

SANDY ELECTS TO STAY WITH HER SISTER for the evening instead of going to John's sweat. Charlene's brief comments earlier this afternoon have suggested there may be some things she might not want to know about. And it is easy enough to bow out. "Nah, but thanks. Next time. I'll help Charlene clean up the kitchen," was her little white lie over the telephone. "More than likely will see you tomorrow anyway. I think Uncle Gabriel wants to take all of us to bingo. Says it's a fundraiser at the community hall."

Besides, her reasoning is half true. They are tidying up. Sandy snickers watching Charlene cover the leftover stew. She's run out of plastic wrap. So she uses a shower cap. A thin one like something a paying guest in a hotel room would be offered. And those potatoes? There weren't any left to fry in the morning. Enjoyed by all and piled high next to the succulent moose—the most tender meat Sandy's ever eaten.

After a quick clean up, the two sisters take Misty for a walk again. Lucky dog. The light is dim as the last bit of sunlight peeks through the tops of trees, "Yes, you don't spend too much time walking alone out here, especially as it's getting dark. Unless you know the land."

"Why? Something to be afraid of?"

"Well, there are big predators in the bush. Wild cats, wolves, bears. But when Kohkum was alive, she'd always tell me that if you sense someone or something walking behind you and you are not sure who or what it is, don't look back."

"Why did Granny say that?"

"Could be the Bushman."

"What's that?" Sandy's is intrigued and she wishes was carrying a notebook. She would have used it. Charlene tells her a story about a mythical creature a little like Bigfoot.

"Kohkum told me that if children are bad, Bushman eats them. If people are bad, he takes them when they are out on the land—never to be seen again. If you hear him walking behind you, pray and he might leave you alone. Because he himself is not all bad. Just a reflection of what is in our own hearts.

"Kohkum told me, he protects those who are good. That's his role. To eliminate the bad and protect the good. And, you can't hide from him." Sandy loves the story, knowing it's a fable meant to encourage respect, being helpful and being kind to each other. It is here that Sandy realizes the Bushman is in all of us. Darkness or light? Choose wisely.

She wants to ask Charlene about the Centaur and if she knows any legends about him. She wants to ask if Charlene has ever seen anything like the half-man/half-elk? But they are interrupted by the sound of footsteps behind them. Bushman? Centaur? They don't look back.

Eerie. Especially when little Misty reacts as she did earlier in the trip. A short little yap like she's waiting for someone familiar to emerge. Sandy holds her breath, afraid to turn her head.

Until Maynard calls out, "Hey you two, wait up. I'll walk with you."

12. CHARLENE

A WHOLE LOT OF TEA DRINKING goes on in this cabin. Always wihkaskwapoy. Sandy is definitely taking some of the wild and dried mint leaves home with her when she heads back to the city. The smell of pine wood burning in the stove creates a warmth for heartfelt conversation to finally begin. Charlene spoons another heaping spoon of sugar in her tea. Sandy prefers it just the way it's brewed.

"So, I haven't had a whole lot of time to ask you much," Sandy says. She has so many questions. "No nieces or nephews for me from you?" She doesn't like the way she's phrased this question. Like she is prodding someone during an interview. "You are just such a beautiful woman, Char. Never been married?"

Of course she has been. Some time ago. Found the love of her life. Charlene explains. "I fell in love with William the moment we met. I know so many people don't believe in love at first sight. But I know they are wrong. It happens." She continues.

So many people who belong to Peter Ballantyne Cree Nation were disenfranchised and forced to relinquish their Indian Status in order to get a job with the provincial government. And they had to get a job. The government had built a dam. No consultation. They simply moved on in, bulldozed and destroyed, to create water power from the mighty Churchill River. The land, which since time immemorial had sustained the people of the Cree Nation, was flooded. The fish they relied on for sustenance were poisoned. And species like the black sturgeon all but disappeared. Even the plants they used to harvest were now under water. Some stories are about people who drowned because the flooding happened so quickly and without notice. Many were not prepared to evacuate. But there is little written evidence of this. Only stories that have been remembered and passed down. "Old Mooshum used to provide our family with everything we needed, until this flooding happened."

But there were still mouths to feed so Mooshum did what he had to do and he took a job at that very dam site. And he had to give up his Indian Status if he wanted to be called an employee and if he wanted to get paid so he could buy food for his family.

"It wasn't until after Mooshum had passed that so many of us realized that we do still have rights. I became one of those fighting for change and for finding ways to be reinstated."

Even though Charlene is trained as a nurse, she talks about embarking on the fight to try and regain their status rights. She'd heard about William, the lawyer. He was the first Saskatchewan Cree to be trained and called to the Bar. She phoned him to set up a meeting and then drove to Prince Albert to talk to him. "And that was that. We were inseparable from the very moment we met." They were married within a year, but mostly living apart because of their work.

They coped and found ways to stay close and connected in spite of the distance. William wrote her poetry, sending it in the mail almost daily. She reaches for a file folder that sits just underneath the albums of old photos the two have been going through. Charlene manages a gentle smile as her memory goes elsewhere, then shares with Sandy William's beautiful words, written on handmade parchment paper. The sentiment and warmth of this moment makes Sandy cry.

Charlene chokes up when she tells Sandy that it all ended one night and that she has never recovered. Never will.

William was driving the northern roads at night, commuting from Prince Albert to see her. Maybe even speeding a bit because he had something substantial to share. But he was never able to share the news. A logging truck—with a tired driver perhaps—pulled out into his lane on icy roads. William swerved. His car rolled and ended up impaled by several of the logs. Charlene's husband died immediately.

"If it wasn't for our cousin Maynard, I don't know if I could have made it through that terrible time. He stayed with me for weeks. I stopped eating and it was Maynard who was there to physically spoon-feed me. He sat by my bed and read books to me. Don't even remember what he read, I just remember his voice. He'd comb my hair and dry my tears. He forced me to take walks with him just to make sure I'd get outside once in a while."

"I love hearing that. Wish I could have been there for you too, Charlene," Sandy holds her sister's hand as Charlene revisits that painful night.

"The RCMP came to my door to inform me of the accident. They gave me a package that was found on the passenger's seat. A plain cardboard box, unwrapped. Inside was a pair of hand-stitched baby booties. They were made of soft leather and still smelled of smoke tan."

Charlene says she found out later that her husband was coming to tell her that he'd made junior partner. All this driving back and forth would be coming to an end because his salary was being increased and she could quit her job at the Health Centre. He wanted to finally start a family.

"I keep the booties beside my bed. They still smell of smoke tan. And I miss him every single day." Their love remains.

Since William's death, she has remained in anguished silence and has never spoken freely. Charlene is surprised that she has been so open about her feelings. She's always kept her feelings and emotions private and buried. A snippet of how she feels sometimes makes its way to Maynard's ear. But rarely so. Mostly her feelings are truths whispered only to the wind.

Somehow sitting here with Sandy, her sister, has provided her the safety to reveal and release the deep and private emotion she continues to feel: a profound sadness.

Through tears, Charlene tells Sandy that even as she was grieving and making funeral arrangements, another poem arrived. William had sent the letter the same day he'd left the city, before the accident that took him away forever.

You took my name
it's where we both belong
me by your side
you—a part of me
turning to each other
in times of need
strength
love and joy
those times are many.

I have been waiting for you
a lifetime.

I thank Creator that you
are now here.

Wherever you are
Is where I belong
where you are
is where I grow strong.

I am your husband
been waiting for you
all of my life
and forevermore
I cherish you
my wife

You have brought light
to places once dark
you have helped me
to finally
open my heart

beside you
my safety
laughter and growth
rest in the shelter of your love

Charlene says she can never replace his memory with another.
Will never. Never.
   Now, it is Sandy's turn to wipe away tears.

13. BINGO

WIHKASKWAPOY FIRST THING in the morning up north. The smell of the mint is sweet in contrast with the earthy reminder of burning sage—smudging has become Sandy's morning routine. Has been ever since meeting Old Joe Bush Sr. a couple of years ago. She's appreciative, but isn't in need of the small bundle John gave her the other day. She's brought her own with plenty to spare, which she intends to leave behind.

But Sandy is a late riser this morning. Uncle Gabriel has been chopping and stacking wood since before dawn. The Old Man hardly perspires anymore, he's so used to the lifelong activity. And always in the same overalls or green work pants. Sandy wonders if he's ever worn a pair of jeans.

Maynard has been up for some time too. Baking. A couple dozen cupcakes sit on the table, already decorated. Fig squares and a raisin pie. He respects Sandy's desire for offering morning gratitude with her smudging and doesn't say anything, nor does he interrupt, until it's obvious she is done.

"Hungry?"

"Sure. Pancakes again?"

"Cha. I made something special," Maynard spoons a warm, heaping spoonful of berries, brown sugar, and oatmeal in a bowl. Sets it in front of Sandy, and says, "The blueberry harvest was amazing this year. Never seen so many. And sweet. Try it." He smiles.

"Kind of like a blueberry crisp?"

"Well, I like to think of it more like porridge à la Maynard!" He winks and goes to the fridge. "And put some of this on it. Heavy cream. Milk is too boring for my special porridge."

Sandy sniffs the breakfast offering. It's heavenly and will surely live in the warm memories she is collecting from this place. When she lifts a spoonful into her mouth, she's speechless and can only make light grunting sounds indicating her pleasure.

"Knew you'd like it. My mom taught me."

They both hear Charlene as she comes down the hallway and then enters the room. Her eyes are a bit puffy, but she manages a smile. Sandy knows that remembering her husband last night could not have been easy. Charlene had been sobbing most of the night. Sandy heard her crying and she feels honoured that Charlene opened up to her, allowing herself to be vulnerable.

"I know you made mint tea, cousin. But it feels like a coffee morning for me," Char admits.

Maynard reaches for the old percolator on top of the stove. "Have some brewing right here. Sit cousin. I will pour you a cup and get you a bowl of my berry breakfast." The heat from the wood stove rushes out when Uncle Gabriel opens the door. He's carrying an armful of logs that he arranges neatly near the stove. He shakes a bit of snow from his work gloves, hangs up his coat, and joins everyone at the table.

"A goddamn son-of-a-bitch out there today. Holy. Cold." He doesn't even have to ask and Maynard brings him a cup of mint tea and some berry breakfast. "Oh, this is good. Smells just the same as when my beautiful wife would make it." He enjoys a spoonful, "But what's up with the apron, my boy? Makes you look like a sissy."

Tension suddenly fills the space that only moments ago was occupied by peace, warmth, and familiarity. "Ah, Dad. You know the water truck runs less frequently in winter. Thought I'd save my clothing from dough and flour so I don't need to do so much laundry."

"Is true," Uncle Gabriel nods, tilting his head towards the

counter top where all the baked items are set to cool. "Those for supper tonight?"

"Nah, Dad. For the bingo this afternoon. You know that."

Charlene seems to have no appetite for even a special breakfast. She informs everyone that she feels like a bit of time to herself. She excuses herself from the table, grabs Misty's leash, then pulls on her winter gear and the two head out for a walk. Sandy understands her sister's need for a few quiet moments. Her departure signals an uncomfortable lull, but for the crackling of the wood stove. Why is it someone always feels the need to fill the space in moments like this? This time around it's Sandy who notices the old photo album still on the small table beside the couch. She slurps her now-cooled wihkaskwapoy and moves towards the family room to get it. She is intending on asking some questions. But just as she's setting her chair aside, a mouse runs out from under the couch.

"Ugh! Apakosis!" Maynard shrieks. Instead of doing something to kill the rodent, like grab a broom, he becomes frantic. He jumps up onto a chair. Sandy makes a dive for the couch so her feet are not sharing the floor with that mouse. Uncle Gabriel is calmly watching the goings-on and finishing up his berry concoction when the door flings open wide.

Another blast of cold air enters the room and with it the hulking silhouette of John Wayne, who notices the kerfuffle. "What in God's good name is going on here?" The mouse starts running in circles, instead of making a straight line to wherever it may have originally been going, likely towards the berry breakfast. Too bad for apakosis. The heel of one of John's heavy Sorel winter boots turns it into a victim. *Thud.* The sound of crushing bones and what looks like jelly on the floor now are all that's left of the little intruder.

"Jesus, Maynard! You are acting like a girl. Get down from there," John Wayne mocks. "Holy. Ever since you were a boy, you've been afraid of mice." John lets go a sinister laugh that reeks of dominance and malice.

14. MYRNA

AFTER THE MOUSE IS TOSSED into the trash, Uncle Gabriel excuses himself. Breakfast is done and he's going to stack more wood before bingo, he says. But that's not it. He's already stacked enough for two seasons. What he really craves is quiet reflection, not that a man like him would ever admit to this. But the cabin is small. Not a lot of room for private thoughts.

It's his second winter without her. His Myrna. He thinks, *I knew her my entire life.* And indeed he did. Slowly forcing each step towards the woodshed, he can still see her face, remembering the first time he laid eyes on her.

She is so small and brown. Just six years old and in her first year of many attending the same residential school as he. Her black hair has just recently been cut. The edges are still jagged. Her bangs are crooked. He watches as she does her best to choke back tears and the stale cardboard-tasting meal in front of her. From way across the room, Gabriel notices that the spoon she's holding is almost too big for her small hands. In this ungodly room, called the dining hall, which always smells more of bleach than food—Gabriel finds a friend for life. He knew this at that very moment. They met in residential school and in that way, they'd really been together all their lives. Even though they were never able to spend time together as children because the girls were kept to one side of the dining area, one side of the playground, and one side of the dormitory. Still they found each other.

Even death cannot break that bond.

The Old Man stops before reaching the wood shed and decides instead to take a walk. Freshly-fallen snow means he can follow Charlene's footsteps. It'll be good to walk with his niece on this fine day. And Misty, who reminds him of the first dog that Myrna talked him into bringing home so many years ago, even though he didn't want to.

They were driving home from Prince Albert. Married less than a year, when Myrna sees a cardboard sign written with black letters. Free Puppies. Just outside a farmyard on the highway. "Oh, come on, nicimos. Stop. Please." Myrna only calls him sweetheart in Cree when she really wants something. She looks over at him and touches his knee. And in this moment, Gabriel doesn't see his wife. He sees a little girl. The one he met so many years ago. It is mere seconds before the old pickup comes to a halt and is forced into reverse gear. The litter is a large one so Myrna has many pups to choose from. But she goes for the runt. The one at the edges of the box that every other pup seems to neglect. A male pup just recently weaned.

This is what Misty reminds him of. The first little joy in their lives. They named him Salt. Short for Salt of the Earth. Sandy's Misty is the same size as Salt. Same colouring. Same playful temperament and she brings back loving memories.

Gabriel remembers how holding Salt would always make Myrna feel happy and sad at the same time. They'd been trying, he and Myrna. And having fun too, trying to make a baby. The little cabin he still lives in had only two rooms back then. More have been added since.

As he walks amongst the black spruce, Gabriel recalls the first time he thought they'd be a family.

Myrna is so happy. Beaming. She finds some cloth material in town to make a cradle board—a portable baby carrier. She asks Gabriel to go find some wood because she has a few pieces of scrap leather left over from the last time she made him some gloves. Even though he's supposed to be checking traps, he changes his plans to find the perfect pieces of pine. By the time he returns home, Myrna is on the floor. She is surrounded by blood and crying. The baby went away.

It happens more than once. The joy and ecstasy of a newly-wed couple learning they'd conceived, followed by death and despair. And in those moments when Gabriel had to leave—to hunt or fish so they stayed fed—it was Salt who watched over Myrna. Salt is the one she'd hug when no baby was able to stay for long.

By the time Maynard is finally conceived, Myrna doesn't even tell her husband. She waits three moons, counting her blessings. When baby is still growing inside on the fourth, she finally tells Gabriel. Months later, a strong, healthy son is born. He is delivered by Kohkum who is a midwife, in the very room where Maynard still sleeps today. They name him Maynard, honouring the memory of Gabriel's Mooshum.

Gabriel thinks about the origins of Myrna's name, which means peace. And the origins of his own name: Archangel Gabriel. A name with purpose. A name meant to clear away confusion and obtain the confidence to act on decisions. Associated with the raising of children.

Has he failed his peaceful wife's memory by recoiling earlier this morning? Accepting his child's different ways of doing things? Aghast that Maynard would wear an apron? Embarrassed that Maynard fears a scampering mouse?

He's always been so proud of his only son. Maynard, who has been checking traps with him since his first tooth fell out. He learned to bow hunt with his cousin John Wayne by the time he was ten. Brought more than one buck home. Maynard, who was one of a handful of kids in the area who graduated from Grade Twelve. Went on take some business management courses and had a good job with the government.

But since coming home from Prince Albert, since Myrna's death, he's been different. Or maybe he's always been like this and Gabriel just didn't notice. Still stands on a chair because he's afraid of a mouse. Gabriel thought he'd outgrow that behaviour. Regardless, Maynard deciding to stay home after Myrna's passing has been a godsend once again. The Old Man would have been crazy with loneliness. Can hardly make it through each day without his love, Myrna. Forever in love.

It's in this moment, Gabriel hears Misty's familiar bark just around the bend and not too far ahead. While reminiscing, he's done something no northern hunter should ever do, which is to not pay attention to his surroundings, to what the land is telling him. As Gabriel walks towards Misty's frisky yelps he notices three sets of footprints.

Clearly, one is Charlene's and her new-fangled boots that Sandy brought for her from the city. The other is Misty's familiar paw prints. The third he doesn't recognize. Cloven but also horse-like. And unlike anything he has seen in all his years.

15. MARY ANN

EVERYONE WITHIN A HUNDRED KILOMETRES has taken the time to make the drive to bingo. The small community hall in Deschambault has been bursting more than once. Now, there are no more fears, and no more raids in the night when women are not protected. Or maybe it's just an illlusion. Maybe those Narrows of Fear—Wapawikoscikanik—still exist. Maybe in a different way?

There is a smell to this community hall that Sandy will always remember, storing it in her memory like a gem. Sweet baking assembled with love and care. Now she knows why Maynard spent so much time with the oven earlier this morning.

For the most part, the bingo prizes that are given out are baked goods and not money. Prizes of pie and cookies and squares. The actual grand prize is one hundred dollars for a black-out winner. A two-dollar bill gets anyone in the door to play and proceeds go to youth recreation. But it's the friendship everyone really comes for, which is worth a whole lot more. Plus there is always an impromptu feast that isn't advertised but everyone knows it will happen.

As the Bingo Master loads his balls and counts his cards, women arrive with plates of meatloaf and potatoes. Fish and wild rice. Jelly salad and bannock. Everyone eats before the game begins. They laugh until the rafters can barely hold any more.

Within the hour, everyone is seated and ready for the game.

But it seems like there is always someone who feels the need to make a pompous entrance and call attention to himself. Not surprisingly, as everyone is seated and ready to begin play, the big doors to the hall fly open. John Wayne saunters in. Rarely by himself. Always with someone new on his arm.

"Oh, for Christ's sake," Charlene groans. "Here we go again."

Sandy remembers why Charlene doesn't attend the sweat lodge ceremonies that John has been conducting. "Can't really believe him," she said. "I know his past. But more importantly, I know how he is acting." Char believes, but does not say aloud, that John's new addiction involves living a charade. Wanting praise. Craving it. More concerned about public perception than his private actions. She wonders why he doesn't he realize that people talk, People have long memories. They all remember.

Cloudy days and drunken nights. Fighting. Cheating. Lying. It's John's past. He talks about it only to say he's conquered it, "I am sober and healthy."

Depends who you talk to.

John is proud to say, "I didn't need to go to A.A. or anything like that. Did it myself. Went to sweats three times a week." And what did he do there? Offer prayer—which is good—but doesn't always get to the heart of problems without truly facing demons and frankly discussing issues with the others in the sweat lodge, with the Elders. Being honest and real.

"So now, I run sweats too. I am trained to conduct ceremony. We all need to return to spirit."

Nice talk—always boasting about truth and love and forgiveness. And he is convincing. Until you meet his ex-wife. He left her shouting, "I'm outta here." Never explained why. He stormed out after she'd criticized his behaviour. Just once. She became homeless for a time. He left her with a mountain of bills, an ocean of accusations, and three kids. He never offered any financial support.

How he's treated her is a true indication of who he really

is Char believes. Sandy agrees. No matter his words today. Wapawikoscikanik. At the narrows of fear.

Almost immediately, John Wayne shacked up with a young lady he met at one of the sweats he ran. Dangerous times to cross that line of being someone's spiritual advisor and then take her to bed. Sounds too much like the abuse in residential schools.

It didn't take long for him to start treating her badly too.

They were at a pow wow. John had started to dance. And with that he promptly started to spurt out teachings of respect as though he was reciting some passage in a book—not written by him.

After intertribal, when everyone is invited to dance, John took off his feathers and set them on two chairs. "We must respect our feathers and the spirit of the eagle. The eagle is the only one who is able to fly highest in the sky, and in that way, take our prayers to Creator." But, for all his talk about the sacredness of women in his sweat lodges, he's left his new woman with nowhere to sit. She is forced to sit on the cold concrete floor in front of him. Then he makes her get coffee for him as the night becomes longer.

That was a while ago.

He's got a new woman now. A young one again. Her name is Mary Ann. John makes her walk seven steps behind him.

What's up with that?

16. MERRY ANN?

HER MEMORY OF SO MANY DETAILS of her life is vague or even non-existent. Maybe she is blocking them and convincing herself that things didn't happen the way she thinks they did. Is it a coping mechanism? She does remember her feelings though: terror, too many times.

Mary Ann has never opened up enough to allow the feeling of closeness and being loved by family. Nor has she harvested any real friendships. Maybe she has built a wall around herself to protect herself. From what?

Revenants of the past. Was it a dream or something that really happened?

Mary Ann recalls trauma and screaming and being ripped from someone's arms. This is a recurring memory. Was it her mom's arms? Mary Ann never met her mom. Or maybe she did? She doesn't even know if the memory is real. Something she may have read? Seen on television? Something someone told her? Or just her imagination? But one thing is certain. She was taken from the dream and grew up in a bad place.

Her memory of other moments are just as vague.

She has a new brother when she arrives at her new home. His name is Jake. Five years older. He hates her. Has ever since the day she joined this new family that adopted her. They all have white skin. Hers is brown.

But brother Jake always waits to show his bad feelings. When no one is looking he pulls Mary Ann's hair. And, when they are away from home and in the school yard, when she is being called "shit for skin" and teased to the point of crying, he is silent. Often smirking. Or even joining in.

To this day, she hates olives. Even the sight of them. It's because of Jake. She remembers being at a family picnic one summer. Jake finds some deer poop. Scoops one up with a tissue that's in his pocket. "Here," he says, offering her the small, dark tidbit. He tells her, "It's like a pickle. Called an olive. You'll like it." He falls to the ground, laughing so hard, when the little Mary Ann almost chokes, gagging to get rid of the taste of shit in her mouth.

By the time Mary Ann is twelve, she spends quite a bit of time alone. Her parents are away from this large bungalow home more than they are in it. Their dad is at the golf course way too often. Her mom started taking classes to upgrade her cooking skills. Except she never really seems to cook anything new. Just wears new lipstick, a new hairdo, and new dresses. Like their dad would even notice. The two hardly even talk anymore. But, today she says, "Jake is around to babysit if you need anything, Mary Ann. He's close by. And there's always the phone."

Early autumn. A Saturday afternoon.

Jake is out playing volleyball. There is a tournament today. He's grown big and strong and is a good spiker. Her mom and dad are gone, "but there are leftovers in the fridge." Mary Ann is in her bedroom, listening to the radio. It's disco and Donna Summer's "Bad Girls" is at the top of the charts.

Mary Ann grabs a bottle of cologne from her wooden dresser. There is pink liquid inside. The clear glass bottle is shaped like a skinny flashlight. The perfect shape to pretend it's a microphone.

Every weekend, she looks forward to the local newspaper printing lyrics to The Top Ten Songs of the week. Mary Ann splays the open pages across her bedspread. The black and white newsprint is in sharp contrast to her bright pink bedspread, which is decorated with images of white carnations.

She puts the perfume bottle up to her mouth, studies the words to the song and sings those words to her favourite teenage heartthrob of that year. There is a poster of *Happy Days* television star Scott Baio above her headboard.

Her happy moment is snapped in half. Jake has returned from his game. Maybe he never left. Just waited until their parents were gone. Intent on causing harm? Turns out he was.

Her memory is spotty. But she remembers the feeling: terror, too many times.

And being ripped.

Normalized dysfunction. Maryann has been abused so often and for so long that she thinks it is normal behaviour for men to hit. To belittle. To demean and be mean to our women. Sadly, Mary Ann doesn't even recognize this as abuse. But it is. And it's why—even if John Wayne treats her badly—she'll accept it. He says he loves her. Normalized dysfunction.

Where are our warriors?

She is likely wearing a ribbon skirt.

17. THE NEXT MORNING

JOHN WAYNE BURSTS OPEN THE DOOR to Gabriel's cabin—like he always does—without knocking. But he doesn't come empty-handed. Carrying a chocolate Bundt cake that he won at bingo yesterday. And walking behind him, the new young girlfriend, Mary Ann.

Sandy is happy to see her again. There is something familiar about her. But Sandy doesn't want to ask. Where do you start? Just something familiar. The time will present itself. For now, breakfast.

As he often does, Maynard has prepared a stack of pancakes for everyone. Served with birch syrup that he, himself, tapped and processed. "We make the most of what the land has to offer." Sandy expects a bitter taste and is pleasantly surprised when the sweetness is like a mixture of maple syrup with an edge that speaks of ruggedness. Like driving on a northern road with the windows down in winter.

"I'll do the dishes. Wonderful meal. Thanks cuz." Sandy feels like she's being doted on and needs to express her gratitude for a wonderful visit. Besides, it's clear Maynard wants to be elsewhere than in this kitchen right now. He seems so melancholy. Even the sweetness of conversation and syrup can't take off the edge.

"Gonna go set some snares. Maybe get a rabbit for dinner." Maynard heads out the door. But maybe getting a rabbit isn't really his intention.

As he heads outdoors, he thinks, "There's something about a fresh snowfall. Like being able to start something brand new. No tracks to follow." Maynard steers his snowmobile away from the land. He's heading out on the ice. No rabbits there. But something for him? He hopes.

He wonders if the young sandwich salesman might still be visiting? He hasn't been able to get him out of his mind so he'll drive around for a bit to see if he might recognize his contraption. "What am I doing?" Maynard asks himself. "What'll I do if I find him?"

He knows what he wants to do. Start a fire in the wood stove in the ice shack. Lay down a blanket. And lay down with the young man. He wants to run his fingers across the gentle outline of his face. Smell his hair and put his tongue at the nape of Shad's neck. Run his tongue across the boy's chest. Probably doesn't even have chest hair. He longs to feel the strength of his Sir Duke. That's what he'll name that glorious spiked wonder. Longs to dance with Sir Duke and taste Shad's salty lava in his mouth. Maynard feels a twinge of guilt. He's beginning to swell and get hard.

But there are no fresh tracks on the ice. And no one to witness. Just whiteness and cold. He stops his snowmobile. Takes off his gloves and puts his hands inside his pants. In these moments, he wears nothing but thoughts of his desire. This isn't the first time he's pleasured himself out on the land. His cum freezes almost as soon as it hits the ground. Just satisfaction twinged with want and desire.

He thinks maybe he'll set a snare after all. No sense in wasting the day. But, glancing across the land, he can't help but feel like he's being watched. But by who?

18. INDISCRETION

THE TIME FOR REFLECTION has come to an end, and the Old Man has made his way back to the cabin. It's warm and it smells like home.

Charlene smiles, hands Gabriel a cup and he savours his coffee. Just one big mug each morning. He drinks it with a bit of milk. Stopped using sugar some time ago when his diabetes began to cause problems. Gabriel is enjoying his visit with Sandy and Charlene. Nice to have women in the house again.

"Uncle? Do you want me to top up your cup?" Char holds the coffee pot in the air and Gabriel nods affirmative. He will have a top up. It's a special day. He loves how the women fuss over him, reminds him of younger days.

Gabriel removes his false teeth, holding them in his hand. It causes both women to snicker as Charlene readies the ingredients for hamburger soup. Just in case Maynard does not come back with a rabbit. "Uncle!" she chides, "why did you take out your dentures?"

"Because I am remembering a story from a long time ago. You made me laugh so hard when you were a little girl. I've had false teeth for so long, I don't even remember having real teeth. But yes, when you were little Charlene, I took my dentures out once and you told me a story. I have never forgotten. You were maybe only seven years old at that time."

Gabriel's smile is wide as he recounts how Charlene as a young girl used to believe that when a child's tooth fell out it would get recycled. She believed that dentists would reuse those baby teeth and turn them into dentures for the elderly.

"Well, it's not surprising that my imagination was so active. My mom and Auntie Myrna used to tell me stories all the time." Charlene tells them how every year she looked forward to baking Christmas cookies. "Our mom used to tell me legends about how we came to this earth while we baked. When we'd make star-shaped cookies, she would say, "In our culture, the Old Ones always told a story about The Star People. They said it's how we came to be here on this Earth. They say Creator sent our People down to Earth on a spider web. We come from the Heavens."

The story prompts Sandy to take out some ingredients for more baking. "We can have sugar cookies anytime of year. Not just at Christmas. Continue to talk. I'll prepare some cookies. With sweetener of course."

Uncle Gabriel takes another sip of his coffee and raises his mug at that suggestion. Charlene keeps talking. "She always used to tell me stories. When we would bake gingerbread men, mom would talk about the Little People."

In case Sandy hadn't heard, Charlene explains, the Little People are spirit beings. "They are assigned specifically to children to keep them from harm. Kind of like Guardian Angels they talk about in church. I used to leave out cookies for them because our mom believed the Little People like to eat candy and sweet things. It was one way to attract them. And to say thanks for keeping us safe."

"Awww, I love these stories," says Sandy, who is wearing Maynard's apron to keep the flour off her lime green sweater. Suddenly the mood changes.

Uncle Gabriel says something uncharacteristically mean, "See? That apron looks good on you, but holy, it bothers me when Maynard dresses like that." Gabriel's tone is again sinister and mocking, which surprises even him.

19. PICKING A SCAB

GABRIEL FEELS SOME SHAME, realizing his harsh comment. He puts his mug on the table and walks to the window. He peers out and makes a statement. "You know what, girls? I can tell by the look of this sky, it is going to be a cold one tonight. There are sun dogs." For the third time this morning, he takes off his comfy slippers that Sandy brought him as a gift and slides his feet into his big, heavy winter boots, "I'm going to make sure we have a good supply of wood for tonight. You two keep baking. I will be back before you know it. Might even do some shovelling." The Old Man slides into his army-green coloured parka that hangs by the door.

Sandy and Charlene wave but say nothing. Hard to believe what just happened. The harsh words Uncle said. It's not like him to be unkind, in any way. In uncomfortable silence, they continue to fashion sugar cookies, which contain no sugar.

Once outside and alone, the Old Man has a conversation with himself.

What the hell is wrong with me? And why am I so hard on my boy sometimes? He's never done anything wrong. God, forgive me for having bad thoughts.

Instead of walking towards the wood shed, Gabriel decides to take a stroll. This time by himself. Lovely day. Cold and crisp. But as he grows older, Gabriel realizes the nightmare that plagues him sometimes even surfaces during the day. Like now.

Brother Thorn is insatiable. Preying on boys. And on girls at the residential school. There is this one time—a hot summer day—when the Brother asks young Gabriel to come with him to pick some blueberries. They'll be part of dessert.

Wanting any nice change from their dull routine, young Gabriel takes a pail and follows Brother Thorn down a path. They don't talk much. It's sweltering and there is a small pond nearby. "Let's take a dip and cool down before we start picking," he tells the boy.

A swim! The perfect remedy.

But neither of them has brought a swimsuit, "It's okay. We can go in the buff. No one needs to know."

"What does that mean? In the buff?"

"Naked."

But there is no swimming in mind—unless you count Brother Thorn's hot sperm up his ass. Sperm swimming towards the sin the Brother has just committed. All young Gabriel can do is cry.

Brother Thorn is never stopped.

It terrifies Gabriel to think his son might have the same darkness within him. Like Brother Thorn. Wanting boys.

20. CHOOSING THE ROCKS

AFTER HIS PANCAKES, John Wayne sets out to ready himself to run another sweat tonight. Like so many others, ceremony has strengthened his spiritual journey. It's helped him to stop drinking. It's helped him with violent behaviour, which was the first place he'd turn in the past.

But there are still lingering shadows. Even as he prepares, he sometimes finds himself questioning faith. The sting of one of his ex-wives when she criticized him for just walking away from the family, leaving them with nothing. It was true. He'd bolted because that's what he'd always done. Didn't talk about problems or even if there were problems. And, if there were, he never talked about a way to work through it all. Instead, fear guided him to flee. That's always been his response. Fear. Flee. And then pretend everything is all right. It's why he conducts the purification ritual two or three times a week. Wash the spirit clean. It's something. The lodge represents the womb of Mother Earth, with the aim of bringing clarity and renewing deep connection with the universe.

This evening though it'll be specific. Mary Ann wants a traditional name so this will be the focus of prayers and offerings.

The winter season is not an easy time to find the proper rocks that will be heated in a large bonfire and brought into the lodge. It's good foresight that he and Maynard collected a large pile in the fall. They are covered with snow now but there will be no need for searching. Just choosing.

He thinks of his own Indian name given to him some years ago. Iskotewi-piyesis Ka-nimihtat. Dancing Firebird. The firebird, some stories say, punishes humans who break moral rules. But it's his name and it gives him a sense of peace knowing that the direction he's going in is a good one. It's also the reason he has started to dance. To honour the name.

But he finds it bothers him when he becomes distracted. He sometimes has unclean thoughts when a young woman, dressed in a nightie with her bare legs comes in. Unclean thoughts. It's something for him to work on.

Moving the heavy rocks closer to where the fire will be set later, John thinks about a name for Mary Ann. She's young. She's lost. She's been hurt too many times before. He knows this because he met her at an Alcoholics Anonymous meeting in Prince Albert. He goes once in a while now—not so much for the meeting—but mostly to find out where the next sober dance will be held.

It is at one of these meetings that Mary Ann burst into tears recalling repeated sexual abuse in the home where she was adopted. A place that was supposed to be safe. He remembers her words and the anguish of admitting that she'd been harmed.

"He shattered my innocence without regard. Dark and ugly is how I felt under those stairs where I knelt. I was just a child unable to talk. And even today it is a difficult walk. To admit being harmed in a place where everyone thought I would be safe."

For all his faults, John Wayne truly wishes to help her. Maybe it'll undo some of the bad things he himself has done.

21. SKINNING

MARY ANN ISN'T ALLOWED to assist in preparing the sweat lodge ceremony. John tells her it isn't a woman's role so he suggests she go back to the cabin and sit with his cousins. She's obedient, as he requires her to be.

Cookies are baked so Sandy serves a plate with some mint tea. Mary Ann doesn't want to seem ungrateful but she'd rather have a glass of milk. Always been a dunker.

It's after she goes to the fridge and pours a glass of cold milk that Sandy notices Mary Ann is wearing a familiar carving. A pendant that is almost exactly the same bear shape that she received from John the first day they met. "Interesting pendant around your neck. Where'd you get it?"

"Oh, John gave it to me. Nice isn't it? Says he carved it himself. I wonder if this means I will be getting some type of bear name tonight?" Mary Ann enjoys the cookies but her comment has caused the conversation to quiet.

It's not Sandy who reacts. It's Charlene who pulls Sandy aside amd whispers, "I don't know why my cousin always takes credit for things he doesn't do. John doesn't carve. Probably picked it up at a garage sale somewhere for a dollar."

"Where is he now?" Sandy asks.

"Out getting ready for tonight's ordinance is my guess. He rarely tells me what he's up to. Never has."

Sandy wonders, "Are you going tonight? It's kind of special. Mary Ann will be receiving a spirit name."

"I don't really believe in that stuff, Sandy."

"Well, it wouldn't hurt. I think it's important for women to support each other. And funnily enough, I brought two ribbon skirts with me. Just in case. You can borrow one. Keep it even."

"No thanks. Think I'll pass. I will support her in my own way." Charlene is interrupted as she glances out the window. She sees Maynard has returned, carrying not one but two rabbits, "No matter what anyone says about my young cousin, he's great on the land. Always coming home with something for me to cook up." She turns her attention to Mary Ann, "Ever skinned a rabbit? I can teach you. You too, Sandy. I doubt you have much opportunity to learn this while living in the city."

Harmony. Camaraderie returns again. There is hamburger soup simmering but Charlene says it can go into the fridge and be eaten tomorrow. Tonight it will be rabbit stew. A time for sharing more new flavours and creating new memories.

It sparks lively conversation. The women start talking about their favorite foods.

"I always like moose with gravy and potatoes. Can't beat it really." Truth be told, Charlene enjoys anything that comes from the land.

"You know. This is an odd thing to admit but when I was just a girl, my favourite sandwich was a noodle sandwich." Sandy giggles.

"What the heck is that?" Her sister needs some details.

"It was when my mom—well, the mom I grew up with— when she'd make chicken noodle soup. I would take a fork and dish out the little noodles. Put them on a couple pieces of bread and smother it with ketchup. Tasted pretty good if you asked me. At least in my memory."

At this point, the very quiet Mary Ann finally reveals something. "That's funny. A noodle sandwich. It kind of reminds me of when I was very little. I hardly remember, but I seem to recall someone making me a mustard sandwich."

Sandy gasps. Now she knows why Mary Ann seemed so familiar from the moment they met.

Her suspicion is further verified when Sandy notices a small birthmark at the bottom of Mary Ann's right earlobe. She remembers remarking to a little girl years ago, *"This looks like the mark of an Angel kiss,"* and then she'd blow on the little girls' neck to make her giggle. Sandy's attention is fixed on that Angel kiss birthmark, now that Mary Ann's hair is pulled back in a ponytail and she hasn't put on earrings before joining them all at the cabin.

22. RECLAIMING

"OH MY GOD! I KNOW YOU. Well, I think I did know you a long time ago." Sandy tries to hug Mary Ann, but Mary Ann recoils. She doesn't like to be touched by people she doesn't know well. Something experience has taught her over the years: kindness is often used as a disguise for something mean and unclean.

The young woman's voice flutters, "What do you mean, you know me? Did we go to the same school together or something like that?" Mary Ann is guessing.

Sandy shakes her head in the negative. "I think it was somewhere else."

To which Mary Ann begins to wriggle uncomfortably before responding, "Hmmm. Well, I am glad to be sitting here with you. But we just met a couple of days ago?" Mary Ann is nervous and tense. She's still holding a sugar cookie in her hand but absentmindedly allows it to drop to her lap. It's an opportunity for Misty who is under the table. The dog gently takes the biscuit from Mary Ann's lap and chews happily. A small diversion from conversation.

Misty's furry face and friendly brown eyes remind Mary Ann of one happy memory from childhood, other than the mustard sandwich. And instead of putting her arms around Sandy, she embraces the small dog. Her mind goes back to the only real friend she's ever had. In all of her life.

Mary Ann didn't grow up in the north. She grew up on

the flat plains of southern Alberta. Farming country and, too often, racist country. But she had a dog when she was a little girl. Angel is what Mary Ann named her. A mutt that was two shades of brown with black paws and floppy ears.

There wasn't a lot of tree climbing in her childhood. There wasn't a lot of swimming either. No big trees. No lakes. Mostly fields of hay and durum.

There wasn't much to worry about on the plains. A lot of gophers. A few small foxes but none of the big predators, like up north. So, as often as possible, Mary Ann and Angel headed out into the fields. No one prepared the little girl for a run-in with a flat-headed bastard. That's what the dad she grew up with called a badger. Because a badger has a flat head. Little Mary Ann saw that bastard one day. And he was mad.

"Hissss! Hissss!" The black and brown devil is brandishing his teeth and slinking along the hard ground in the clearing, as though he's part snake. He growls in a voice that's probably the same as a real lion.

Little Mary Ann is unable to scream as the flat-headed bastard scopes her with his beady, evil eyes. She is frozen with fear as he's almost close enough to cut her open with his sharp claws, which leave deep marks in the earth as he passes over it. The badger's focus on the girl means he's paying no attention to other surroundings in that field. Good thing too. These moments allow Angel, her dog, to take that bastard by surprise, flying in from out of nowhere and grabbing the badger by the neck. Another horrible sound! Hisss! The distraction gives little Mary Ann the courage to run. Run as fast as she can and never look back.

Once she reaches the safety of the farm yard, the moments pass like hours and she cries hard for Angel's well-being. Everyone knows that a badger is capable of killing a dog. She cries hysterically and now it is getting hard to breathe. "Where is she?" The thought of having to ask her dad to go and find her dog's dead body is torture. It is the first time that she understands that praying to God is more than just a concept. Mary Ann falls to the ground, a little pile of despair, sobbing uncontrollably.

Then, just as quickly the trauma disappears.

The girl feels a familiar lick on her hand. Through tear-filled eyes, she sees the warm, brown eyes of Angel, alive and wagging her tail. Angel hung around that badger just long enough to distract him. There was no real battle.

As it should be.

Her eyes are misty now as Mary Ann absentimindedly hands Misty another piece of cookie. She wonders why have there been so many badgers in her life. All her life.

23. REUNITED

AS MAYNARD PUSHES OPEN THE DOOR to reveal his prize, he's clearly pleased with himself, "Ladies! We dine tonight!" Because his smile lights up the room, he can't help but notice Mary Ann is less than enthusiastic, "Hey girlfriend, why the long face?" Mary Ann doesn't answer. And it's clear to Charlene that teaching the women how to skin a rabbit will have to wait for another time.

"Do you remember anyone ever calling you by the name Betsy?" Sandy asks. The young woman is biting her lip, doing her best to remember. Or putting up another emotional shield so as not to remember. No one has asked her such a pointed question before. The query unleashes a hundred buried memories. Again.

It's as clear as the morning sunrise on a cold winter day. Mary Ann realizes she dimly remembers hearing that name, *but I thought it was just a dream.* Her expression turns ashen, reaching for a now half-empty mug of cold tea. Her milk is gone. But, there is no sweetness in where her mind wanders next.

A little girl is forced into a coffin, which is the back seat of a black car. A big, angry hand with thick knuckles slaps her small face with enough force to loosen a tooth. "Shut up! If you don't stop, I'll really give you something to cry about." The angry one slams the car door, locking the little girl inside. The coffin begins to move. The world she knows starts to disappear. She cries and cries. But there is no one around to hear her.

No one pays attention to Mary Ann in this big house that is *always too hot because the furnace is cranked. She's just wo-ken up from an afternoon nap. They call her Mary Ann now. Named in memory of a grandma she's never met but there is a picture of the old lady hanging in the living room. Little Mary Ann is missing a tooth. She runs her tongue over the empty space and grabs her dolly before heading downstairs. The smell of freshly-baked bread is calling. Wiping away sleep from the eyes and snot from her nose, the girl is oblivious to a phantom. Her older brother, Jake—named after his grandpa. He is the couple's biological child but complications during his birth meant no more children for them. It's why Mary Ann is here. Adopted little sister so he can have a sibling.*

Jake is reading an Archie *comic in his room across the hall when he hears his little sister's door creak as it opens. Just as little Mary Ann reaches for the handrail to make her way down to the kitchen, she feels a hard shove at the small of her back. More like a foot than a hand. Mary Ann wakes up at the bottom of the stairwell. Bruising on her chin. She doesn't feel like eating bread anymore.*

Memory: *The schoolyard is filled with bullies again. When Mary Ann goes to church each Sunday her prayers are that they will tire of the pushing and shoving and name-calling. Her prayers go unheard. It is Monday and a trio of boys have cornered her again. This time where the red bricks from the schoolhouse stop and the entryway to the gym begins. The smallest of the boys has brought with him a pencil from the classroom and he starts poking Mary Ann in the arm. His movements are quick like he doesn't want to stand too close to her for too long, in case she swings at him. His dirty blond hair is scruffy, as though he didn't comb it before getting on the school bus this morning. The point of the pencil is sharp and leaves a black mark on Mary Ann's new windbreaker jacket. It is blue. The colour of sadness. The bigger boy grabs her sleeve, "What's this? New coat? I guess your Treaty money must have come in!" He is mocking her. The third boy is quiet and doesn't participate. He stands and watches, cackling though with sinister laughter at each indignation thrown at her. That's when Mary Ann notices another onlooker. It's her brother watching from a distance. There is a smirk on his face. He doesn't step in to help her.*

Childhood is fleeting. For some, it is filled with trauma and it seems like a time that didn't happen at all. Only existing and trying to hang on, hoping the next chapter points to a way out.

She's wearing a training bra now and her mom has given her a book from the catechism class that happens in the church basement before mass each week. The book reads like a how-to on what is expected from a young lady. Impure thoughts are a sin. *Mary Ann's mother doesn't give her advice; she just gives her something to read. Like when she began to menstruate. She handed her a box of pads and a pamphlet she picked up at the doctor's office.*

Dark memories until the light creeps in. Betsy. Searching further, she does remember. Holding hands. Being pushed on a tire swing. Lime Kool-Aid. Laughter. "Is this where my memory of mustard sandwiches comes from?" She closes her eyes, takes a deep breath, and remembers the name. Maybe it isn't just a dream that comes at night?

Betsy. It is the name she used to go by, until she got legally adopted, and was forced to live another life. Mary Ann remembers. And, she vaguely remembers Sandy, although, she's pushed most of her early memories away. But, this one, has remained. If not in details, then in heart memory. She remembers something.

But memories of love can be almost too painful, when it is no longer there. When it is taken away. Betsy? She was loved. Did the same happen when she went into another family and became Mary Ann?"

24. BUSHMAN

ESKAB AY WISS. THAT IS THE TITLE of the man who arranges the rocks for the sweat. Prepares the area for prayer. Collects the wood. Collects the water. Starts the fire.

Not today.

Eskab ay wiss knows something is wrong. Tracks. Unrecognizable and running alongside the dirt path which leads into the bush to a clearing. John Wayne said he had dreamed about this site, which is why it was chosen. Often a sweat lodge is built next to a body of water like a stream, pond, or river. But John always has to be different. He told Eskab ay wiss he wanted a lodge surrounded by a grove of trees. This way no one can see them from the road. Rubber-neckers. The fire would be out of view and protected.

Ever since John returned to the north and to traditional ceremony, he's been criticized. Even his own Kohkum told him, *"It's the devil's work."* Like so many of the old people, Kohkum was force-fed the doctrine of Catholicism when she went to residential school. It forbade traditional spiritual practices and beliefs, calling it pagan and sinful. *"It will send you straight to hell."* Her shame reading like a memo from 1875 when Bishop St. Vital Grandin proclaimed that, *"We will instill in them a pronounced distaste for the native life so that they will be humiliated when reminded of their origin. When they graduate from residential schools, the children will have lost everything, except their native blood."*

The narrows of fear.

Despite the naysayers and to his credit, John is a good pupil. For the most part. Walking the Red Road is what he calls it. Returning to traditional ways, learning and passing on the knowledge. He'd be reverent for those few hours a week, although often continuing with lewd behaviour once the ceremony has ended. And when no one else is watching.

He even uses *going to ceremony* as almost a pick up line with women he meets at the dry dances. Those events are held every now and then for people successfully following the twelve-steps of Alcoholics Anonymous. Those women often end up in his bed. Until the next time, when John will dance with another. Interchangeable women in reality: women he tries on for size and discards just as quickly. Next day he's sitting in a circle, extolling his thoughts on the sacredness of woman.

He never admitted any of this to his teacher, the one conducting the sweats. John only offers information he thinks his teacher might want to hear. How his teacher perceives him to be is more important than how he really is.

His teacher might believe. But not everyone is fooled. No one can hide from Spirit.

Maybe that's why Eskab ay wiss found what he's found today. But he can't figure out how it happened. The lodge itself looks as though it has been picked up and thrown to the opposite side of the clearing. The willows broken beyond repair. But surely it would take several men to do this?

Ashes and logs are scattered, littering the area. Broadcloth that had been tied to trees—as a testament of prayer—has been ripped down, exposing broken branches and trunks torn to a vicious wound.

Eskab ay wiss checks for tire or snowmobile tracks. None. No footprints either. What he does find are odd impressions in the snow. Too big for deer. Different shape than a moose.

25. HOSSENFEFFER

IT IS UNLIKE SANDY TO NOD OFF during the day. But that's what happened. After asking Mary Ann if she remembers anyone ever calling her Betsy, the mood becomes somber. Charlene goes outdoors to begin skinning the rabbits. Mary Ann takes a bath. Sandy sits near the warmth of the wood stove. She doesn't remember falling asleep but is familiar with images that come to her in those moments spent away, where a conscious mind does not travel.

The pain is excruciating and blisters the size of angry raindrops rise immediately. Sandy recoils in agony but it's too late. The flame has already burned its scars of hatred onto her soul, permanently placing its mark on her fingers too. An obscene brand. Burned flesh will gnarl. Eventually resembling the folds of bark on an old tree limb. A constant reminder of this curse evoked today.

"Did you bring the money?" the old witch croaks through the ever-present ailment of laryngitis. The wicked one's hair is stiff and scruffy, the colour of rotted hay. In her right hand, the sorceress holds some stones, jagged and the colour of blood. She motions for Sandy to continue with the ritual.

The smoke from the fire does not linger. It marches in a straight line, up to the tips of leafy deciduous trees that dare to bear witness. The crackling of the blaze resembles the sound of reptiles spitting moments prior to a deadly strike.

Sandy throws personal items into the flame. A lock of hair, bits of food, photographs. A loose particle of her own clothing catches fire and Sandy instinctively reaches to snuff it out, burning her hand in the process. In response, the left hand of the decrepit hag disappears under the layers of grey material that she wears. She pulls out a balm that smells of rotted flesh, encouraging Sandy to put it on the wound and promising, "It will stop the pain. But a scar shall remain." Like some type of seal solidifying an unspeakable pact.

But before she can dress the wound something emerges from the bush.

Sandy is awakened by Misty growling followed by the sound of someone slamming the door to the cabin. It is a frantic Eskab ay wiss, "Where's John?"

"He and the Old Man went to the gas station. Said he needed some supplies for tonight. What's wrong?" Sandy can tell Eskab ay wiss is troubled.

"I can't say and I need to talk to John. When did he leave?"

She tells him it's been a couple of hours. Eskab ay wiss gives a look of exasperation, shakes his head and leaves as quickly as he came.

"What's up with him?" Charlene asks, perplexed and holding the two skinned and gutted rabbits, one in either hand, "Eskab ay wiss ran out of the cabin so fast like something has scared him."

Sandy shrugs her shoulders and then decides it is time to change the mood. She makes a joke, "Well, I'd be scared too if I came face to face with a bush woman whose hands are covered in blood and she's carrying a razor-sharp skinning knife." The comment is followed by a small chuckle and contemplative silence. As though both women have decided that whatever is bothering Eskab ay wiss has nothing to do with them. And they can probably do nothing about it anyway.

"Here let me help you with those." Sandy takes the rabbits

and goes to the cupboard—retrieving an oversized pot for boiling. "And let me cut up the vegetables. Never eaten *hossen-feffer* before." At this statement, Charlene bursts out laughing. She remembers that Bugs Bunny episode from her childhood. "Hossenfeffer." It pleases Sandy to make her cousin laugh. So she begins to sing the words to Rabbit of Seville, "Welcome to my shop. Let me cut your mop. Let me shave your crop. Don't look so perplexed. Can't you see you're next?" Silliness that causes Char to cover her mouth to try and hide her smile, the way a little girl does when she makes a joke that is so funny to her alone that she might end up peeing. Unbridled joy and expression.

It reminds Sandy again of little Betsy. The day she talked about eating so many Saskatoon berries that her poop turned blue.

Again, she wonders. Could Mary Ann be that little girl? Is she her little Betsy? The lost little sister from her own childhood? Betsy arrived as a ward of the system, just like Sandy, and she stayed long enough for the two to form a bond. How do bonds break? Sandy has always believed that bonds are sacred.

Maybe they are.

26. THE SHADOW

A HOUSE FULL OF PEOPLE but he still has needs. Maynard always experiences feelings of guilt when he touches himself. He's heard his dad talk about residential school and *those goddamn no-good sons a' bitches*. It's a discussion that started when Maynard grew into puberty.

It was awkward but a teenaged Maynard brought up the subject of masturbation. Gabriel told his son it is sinful and that the priests used to force him—the young Gabe—to touch himself while they watched. *Fucking faggots*. Gabriel cringes each time he envisions their cold bony fingers groping his innocent young flesh. *If you touch yourself, you are a faggot*. Foreboding and a warning to Maynard. Pleasuring yourself is wrong.

Maynard somehow forgets these words in that moment just before eruption. Like now, hiding behind the woodshed, footsteps away from the family cabin and the women preparing food inside. The only witnesses to his actions, a chickadee and a squirrel. He feels safe thinking he's alone.

That is, until Gabriel nears the shed close enough to see his son waiting on rapture. Oblivious to his surroundings, Maynard does not hear his father's footsteps approach. They are muffled on the freshly-fallen snow. A mild breeze carries sound in the other direction.

The Old Man is making his way to the woodshed to retrieve the big axe. Eskab ay wiss had caught up with him and John on the highway as they were coming home from the gas station. Eskab ay wiss tells the story of finding the ceremony site in ruins. Perhaps it can be rebuilt in time for tonight's sweat. New willows will need to be cut. But not without the proper tools.

Gabriel forgets about the big axe when he catches a glimpse of his own son intent on selfishness and pleasure. The Old Man's mind goes awash with dark memory. Brother Thorn and cold, boney fingers. Sweat oozes from the pores above his greying brow, immediately settling and freezing just below the rim of the rainbow-coloured toque Maynard had knitted for him last Christmas. Charlene taught him how to knit as a way for both of them to pass the time, the early days of her grieving process after her husband dies in a vehicle accident.

A coldness extends to the Old Man's hands making them tingle and then feel numb. The Old Man stops short, frozen in place. Seeing his own son touching himself forces Gabriel to remember how that old priest so often forced the young Gabriel to take that old priest's penis in his own hands and jerk him off. One time, down by the wood shed at the residential school. This time the memory not only causes Gabriel emotional pain, but physical pain as well.

He does his best to hurry back to the truck before an extreme shortness of breath stops him from moving forward. Another anxiety attack? He's experienced it before. When the memories resurface, they haunt him. Gabriel tells himself to breathe deeply, to hold the air in, and then let it out slowly. He remembers counselling sessions where he was advised to use all his senses to get through these moments. Smell the air. Listen to the sound of the wind. Feel the heaviness of old, worn Sorels. His beloved oversized boots that for years have hugged and protected his feet.

Gabriel is practically staggering by the time he gets to the pick up truck. He hears John Wayne muttering obscenities while loading supplies like rope, a tarp, and blankets. He slams the tailgate and sees the Old Man. "You couldn't find the axe?"

Gabriel is at a momentary loss for words, then invents a lie, "It's not there." He clears his throat and glances toward the wood shed. "Maybe the boy took it with him to go check one of his traps."

"It's okay, Uncle," John Wayne assures. "Eskab ay wiss probably has one." He heaves a sigh. "I still can't believe something like this happened. Who would do such a thing?" He motions to Gabriel, using his chin to point towards the truck door. "Let's get over there. See what we can salvage."

27. ROBERTA

IT IS A SAD STATE OF AFFAIRS when a person can number more enemies than friends in their life. This is preoccupying John Wayne's private thoughts now as he locks his hubs into four-wheel-drive. The pathway leading to his ceremonial site is tenuous at the best of times. More so with a fresh coating of snow. The news of its destruction causes him to worry about his neighbours to the west. Was it old Murray who destroyed the lodge?

Does she remember? John certainly recalls but has pledged to never tell a soul. He thought he'd made sure that she would never tell anyone either.

It was a couple of months ago. John knew his neighbour, old Murray, was planning on heading to the bush. Always gone for a week or more. Annual hunting trip. But probably more likely just wanting to spend time out on the land. Murray's young daughter was staying with him. Taking care of her old dad.

John had always fancied Roberta, even though she was young enough to be his own daughter. His first thoughts of her happened one summer not that long ago. Roberta had just turned fifteen. And even though old Murray had never been in favour of his daughter showing her skin, it was a hot day. Roberta was cleaning fish near the river, wearing short shorts and a bathing suit top.

She's eighteen now. Just got out of rehab and with nowhere else to go, she came home. John knew she'd be alone until her father came back from this hunting trip. Wicked opportunity, and he didn't think twice.

Bootleggers are always discreet. So when John drives the fifty kilometers to pick up a forty-ouncer and a case of beer, there are no questions asked. Just an exchange of money for over-priced and illegal goods.

It is twilight when he drives up to Murray's cabin. A light is on in the kitchen and John can see Roberta washing dishes through a large kitchen window that has no drapes. Standing at the open door to the home, he can smell the aroma of fried eggs, butter that has been allowed to burn a bit in the pan, and freshly-popped toast.

"Hi Roberta, good to see you. Smells great," he smiles. "Your dad home?" he asks, knowing full-well what the answer is. He'd run into Murray that afternoon, just as the old man was putting some gas-line antifreeze in his tank and loading up some extra gas in containers.

Roberta has no fear of John. No need to. She has known him all her life. John's even come on fishing trips with her family, when her mother was still alive and her brother still lived at home.

"Hi John. Good to see you too," she smiles. "Come on in." Roberta explained that her dad was away for a few days. "I just made a small supper. You are welcome to stay if you like."

He agrees. "Love to. I haven't eaten yet and to tell you the truth, I'm not sure I have anything in the cupboard even when I do get back home."

He takes off his big boots by the wooden door and hangs up his coat. "Got any tea?"

Roberta laughs out loud, "Well, that's a silly question. There's always tea here." She went to the cupboard near the sink where a pile of clean dishes had been set to dry and retrieved a cup. "You take sugar?"

"Well, normally I do," he says, "but on second thought,

I think I need something strong. Feeling a little congested today," he adds. "Damn, cold making its rounds." It's then John produces the large bottle of whiskey he's been holding behind his back, "If you don't mind, I will have something a bit stronger. Heard that a hot toddy will likely do the trick. Can mix it with tea. Did you want to try one?"

He feigns pouring liquor into his own cup but is generous with Roberta's portion. She sniffs the brew, closes her eyes, and hurriedly drinks down the liquid in two big gulps. John pours her another while offering to stoke up the wood stove. He throws on a couple of extra logs for maximum heat.

Before long, John is sitting on the lumpy couch that has been in the house since the seventies. Its cheap wooden frame is covered in what can only be the remnants dreamed up by a colour-blind designer. Heavy gold flowers, surrounded by the worst shades of yellow and orange. John finishes up the rest of his eggs and toast while Roberta slurs, "Okay if I have another toddy?" She removes her bulky sweater, "Is it getting hot in here?"

"No. It's probably just the tea," he says, adding, "I can pour you another. I'm on my way to the sink anyway. Great eggs." John proceeds to pour more whiskey than tea in her cup. "I can stay a bit longer if you like. We can watch some television."

"Okay," she agrees, knowing that if he left, so too would the bottle leave. It was already half empty.

The Beachcombers are on the tube. Roberta though passes out before any of the TV characters are able to refill their mug of coffee at Molly's Reach. Her legs are splayed out on the couch. The small muscle-shirt she wears under her sweater shows most of her black bra.

John moves her body so she is laying flat on the ugly couch. There is no need to be gentle as he pulls her old, grey sweatpants and her ripped yellow panties off, tossing them both on the floor.

From the back pockets of his jeans he takes out a clothes

pin. Old and worn and made from wood. He pulls the cups of Roberta's bra down, revealing young, perky breasts. He massages one breast until the nipple is hard and erect. Then he clamps it with a clothes pin. The sight of her throbbing nipple causes him to swell. The idea of pain with pleasure has always appealed to him.

John undoes his leather belt, unzips his fly, and spreads her legs. He sniffs her first, then licks her to manipulate her wetness. He uses his thumbs to spread her pink lips before fucking her without her knowledge. But not before placing a condom on his hard hungry shaft.

He swears at her, "You little bitch cunt. You like to fuck. Feel my hard cock." His breathing increases and his eyes roll at the moment of his sin. "Here I come, you sick little bitch. Oh! Here I come."

When he is finished, John removes the condom and walks to the kitchen to find a plastic bag. He wraps the condom with the bag, and then puts it in his pants pocket. He removes the clothes pin from her nipple, which is red and swollen.

But he isn't completely done yet. As he zips up his fly, he walks towards the door and reaches for his parka, which is hanging just next to it. From the large pocket of his coat, John removes a flashlight. "And here's my trophy," he spews, shoving the cold cylinder up her crotch. He moves it in and out with force. "Now I can smell you anytime." He removes the plastic bag from his pants pocket and places the wet flashlight inside with the spent condom. He puts both in the large pocket of his parka.

Before he leaves, he writes Roberta a note and places it on the kitchen table, thanking her for her company and for the eggs. Tells her he's locked the door, "Because you were too tired to finish watching the show and I didn't want anyone coming in while you were sleeping."

He redresses her, making sure her head is resting on a pillow and he covers her with an afghan blanket that's draped over the edge of the couch. He recalls Roberta's mom knitting it years ago as they all enjoyed stories around a campire. But he doesn't leave immediately. Instead, he goes out to his truck and brings back that case of beer, leaving the beers in the fridge for Roberta.

He knows from experience that a two-day hangover is more than likely to fog out any memory. He mutters to himself, "God loves Saints and Sinners—and especially those who are a little of both." He takes one last look at Roberta and John is momentarily shocked when, for a few seconds, Roberta opens her eyes.

He feels no remorse for what has just occurred.

28. DISBELIEF AND THE DEVIL

L IGHT FLURRIES HAVE FALLEN since Eskab ay wiss broke the news about the destruction of the ceremonial site. John Wayne is eager to inspect the damage but also a little afraid at what he's about to find. Mostly he's afraid of why this happened.

The tire tracks from when Eskab ay wiss visited earlier are still visible. But just barely so. Driving into the area there is no indication that anything is amiss. Sparrows and chickadees flutter amongst dried husks that still hang from bare deciduous trees, now leafless and covered in hoar frost. There are still a few seeds left in those husks. The small birds will find them. Two large ravens are perched higher up in that same tree. Slim pickings for them though unless a rabbit happens to run out in front of someone's moving vehicle on the road up ahead. All seems as usual. Until John comes to the clearing.

As Eskab ay wiss described, the lodge itself seems to have been picked up and thrown. Most of it is smashed. John is speechless. He gets out of his truck and walks towards where the lodge originally sat. A circle that now sits empty but for a few indentations in the snow. Places where Eskab ay wiss said he'd seen some kind of mysterious tracks—not footprints. John Wayne checks the ground but sees only the glint of sunlight on freshly-fallen snow. He says a prayer asking for clarity and guidance and glances back at the truck. He notices Gabriel hasn't moved.

It's as though the Old Man is frozen in place, for real or

perhaps just within his mind. John thinks maybe Gabriel is shocked at what they've found here. John doesn't see the sweat pouring down the Old Man's forehead, quickly dampening his rainbow-coloured toque.

John gestures that Gabriel should come join him but there is no movement. John goes to investigate.

"I don't know what's happening, John," Gabriel manages to choke out. "But I am having trouble seeing and my arms hurt. They feel like they are on fire."

"Oh my God! You are having a heart attack!" John is momentarily bewildered as to what to do next, "Here," he says as takes off the Old Man's toque, "try to breathe. Don't worry about this mess. I'm taking you to the hospital!"

John figures it will be at least an hour and a half before they can get to the hospital in Flin Flon. There is no time to stop in anywhere and call for an ambulance. He backs his pick-up from the clearing in the bush and makes it to the highway without incident. All the while, he is praying.

They drive in silence. In these moments, Gabriel recollects.

He sees Myrna, his beloved wife. She is young, wearing an apron and standing by the wood stove. He can smell the moose stew. He remembers Maynard as a young boy and teaching his son how to set traps and pull in nets in the winter. He thinks about the thousands of times he himself has walked to the wood shed never expecting what he'd seen this last time there.

My boy. Committing sin.

The Old Man's chest tightens as his memory opens a wound.

His own young hand, not the one of today that is calloused with wrinkles. A young hand. A boy's hand. His own hand moving back and forth as Brother Thorn moans.

Gabriel thought he'd buried those images.

As they continue the drive, for a fraction of a second, John Wayne finds himself squinting in an effort to get a better view of something he's spied under the cover of brush and just alongside the road. He thinks he sees a larger than usual elk. It is just behind some thick bush as the vehicle rounds a curve on the highway. But there is something different about this creature, which is obscured but still faintly visible. Dark and ominous. It is purposely hiding from view. But still watching him.

It sends a shiver down John's spine. He can't figure out why.

29. DISTRESSING NEWS

THE HAMBURGER SOUP IS TAKEN OFF the menu to to make way for rabbit stew. Thanks to Maynard. The "hossen-feffer" meal is done and smells as good as it looks. A luscious cream sauce, like an Alfredo, dotted with colourful carrots, parsley, celery, potato, and red onion. Charlene is having a hard time stopping herself from plunking in handmade dumplings. But the little pieces of salty dough turn to mush so quickly if they are overcooked, so she waits. She's been making dumplings as long as she's been baking bannock. Nikawiy taught her as soon as she was tall enough to reach the settings on the stove.

"Where is Uncle Gabriel? He should have been home a half hour ago. I hope everything is all right."

"I'm sure everything is fine," says Sandy, even though she too is concerned. She recalls with detail the worried look on Eskab ay wiss's face as he rushed in looking for John Wayne.

Just then they hear a vehicle pull into the yard. "Finally," exclaims Charlene as she begins the process of setting the raw dumplings into the hot stew. "These will be ready in ten minutes. Just in time for Uncle Gabriel to get washed and ready for dinner."

But the Old Man doesn't come in through the door. Instead there is a knock. A worried Maynard says, "What the hell?" as he goes to answer. It is an RCMP officer who explains that John Wayne was stopped speeding on the highway on his way to Flin Flon Hospital. Because of the emergency—and worries about Uncle Gabriel's health—they were escorted. The officer who had stopped John's truck immediately put in radio call to the hospital, and they instructed him to administer aspirin to minimize blood clots. That quick action may very well have saved Gabriel's life. The officer then called the RCMP detachment in Deschambault and they dispatched a rookie to alert the family.

Upon hearing this, Charlene turns off the stew. The dumplings will likely turn to mush now. She grabs a pot holder and places it under the hot pot of stew. Without thinking, she places the meal in the fridge. The young officer at the door agrees to escort Maynard, Sandy, and Charlene—they get ready within minutes—to Flin Flon.

Mary Ann will stay behind. Charlene's left her a few phone numbers and asked her to contact relatives and let them know what's happened. Plus, someone has to stay with Misty.

All agree to take Sandy's vehicle. It has a full tank.

"What could have happened?" Charlene laments. "Uncle Gabriel has always been in such good shape for an old man. He's never been sick a day in his life, except for the usual things like a cold."

"And his diabetes." Maynard clears his throat, adding, "Well, there was that one time when he nicked his leg with an axe. But he refused to go to hospital. Mom ended up dressing it. Even used bear grease on it once it had healed. Said it would stop the scarring."

"Oh, I remember that time," Charlene tries to smile. "Auntie Myrna did the same thing the following summer when Uncle got a fish hook stuck in his hand. Remember? It wouldn't come out and he had to rip that fleshy part between the index finger and his thumb."

"Yes. Bear grease," Maynard muses. "Wish we had some right now."

By the time the trio reaches the hospital, cousin Agnes and her husband Bernie are already in the waiting room. Agnes has brought with her a white rosary and a large thermos filled with sweet wihkaskwapoy.

"Anything is better than this hospital coffee," John Wayne says. He's been at the hospital now for almost three hours.

"You are spot on with that comment, John." Agnes does her best to lessen everyone's worry by offering to fill a cup of the mint tea for everyone. They each accept and it brings a small bit of comfort, that is until the surgeon arrives with news.

30. PRAYER

"ARE YOU THE FAMILY OF GABRIEL BEAR?" the young doctor inquires.

"Yes," Maynard manages. "I'm his son."

"Would you like to find somewhere private to discuss your father's condition?"

"No. This is my family. We should all hear the news."

Young Doctor Price is clean-shaven, polite, and to the point. He explains that Gabriel is stabilized, but still not out of the woods. "We have concerns because of his advancing age. And his diabetes. Something like this is hard on the body, even for healthy seniors like your father," he says looking at Maynard. "Gabriel suffered a massive coronary. It takes a toll on all of the organs, especially since it was a while before medical treatment could be administered. We are doing our best to keep him comfortable. He'll be in intensive care for at least twenty-four hours."

A nurse arrives and lets the family know they are welcome to ask for use of blankets and pillows if they plan to spend the night in the waiting room.

No one is allowed to see Gabriel.

As the hour of midnight approaches, a couple more relatives arrive. Charlene introduces Sandy to her Auntie Alex and Uncle Bev, who aren't related by blood but are considered part of the family nonetheless. They drove in from their cabin at Jan Lake. They ask if anyone has a deck of cards. "No," Sandy says, and then remembers, "but I do have that word game—Quiddler—in my glove box."

"Never heard of it," says Maynard, "but I can go out and grab it if you want. Better than just sitting around worrying."

While he's gone Sandy explains it's a game similar to Scrabble. "You make up words with the letters you pick on the cards." But their game is short-lived when Agnes draws letters too ominous for the situation.

D—I—E are the letters she's chosen.

No one speaks a word until Charlene suggests, "Maybe we should all just watch some television." With the wihkask-wapoy all gone, and Agnes saying her rosary twice already, the visitors begin to nod off in the uncomfortable waiting room chairs.

All the while, Gabriel lays sedated in a hospital bed in the intensive care, hooked up to monitors and an IV. He falls in and out of dreams. At least he thinks the images are dreams. They seem so real. One makes him happy.

Myrna is sitting in the steel chair beside his bed. She is a young woman again. Fresh-faced with her long black hair in soft curls that line the top of her white buckskin dress. There is a floral design of beadwork on the sleeves and along the neckline. Gabriel smiles at her, remembering it is the same dress she wore on the day of their wedding. Myrna smiles back, sand says, "Hello, my love. Ready to come home?" She gently takes his hand, raises it to her lips and kisses it. "Astam. Come," she says. "We should go for a walk. Like we used to."

He wants to follow her. But instead monitors start beeping and nurses run into the room. "Call the doctor! Code Blue." Within a minute, the young Dr. Price is massaging Gabriel's chest and orders another injection of nitroglycerin. Another emergency averted. The Old Man rests easily again. His breathing has returned to normal but he hasn't regained consciousness. The medical team leaves.

Myrna does not leave. "What's troubling you, my love? Why are you in here? I am happy to see you but I didn't expect to for some time yet."

As his vision continues, Gabriel talks about his shame. Something he never fully admitted to her the entire time they were married. He weeps and she dries his tears, and says, "You must forgive yourself. It was never your fault."

Then Gabriel's last confession, "Of all the gifts you ever gave me, other than your love, the greatest gift has been our son. But now I find myself ashamed of him, too." He explains that he saw Maynard touching himself. And that he fears he is a homosexual, which must also mean he is a pedophile like Brother Thorn.

"No," Myrna reassures him. "There is no similarity. There is no connection. Maynard is a man. A good man. Our son. He lives with two spirits and understands both. It's our son's gift, my beloved Gabriel, and never a source of shame. And it's something I have always known. " She holds out her hand again and this time Gabriel takes it. The two begin to walk along the pathway leading into the bush behind their cabin. Gabriel notices they are being followed by Salt. Their beloved dog. He's a young, spry pup again, running from tree to tree, gleefully looking for squirrels.

They walk without speaking but communicating even so. It leads Gabriel to a place of peace, love, and acceptance. A place with no judgement or shame.

He knows it is a peace not only meant for him, but also for his son. He longs to tell Maynard but cannot. He has waited too long.

The light beckons and Gabriel follows his beautiful wife.

The heart monitor flatlines, leaving nothing behind but silence.

PART II
THE STRENGTH OF WOMEN

31. CATHEDRAL

MISTY IS A LITTLE WONDER. Always happy. Always ready to go. Each time Charlene feels saddened, she takes Sandy's pup for a walk. These days it means strolling through Regina's rich with culture Cathedral Village neighbourhood where Sandy lives. Uncle Gabriel's death affected Charlene deeply. Opening the wounds of losing her beloved William too soon.

She realizes that the things she's been doing to keep herself busy since her husband passed are really just things to do to make it through another day. No joy. Just routine actions that still lead to sadness at the end of the day.

Doing things just to fill up the space. Learning to knit. Watching cooking shows on TV and substituting wild meat for beef. Keeping her home impeccably clean—not because of a need for tidiness, but because it's a way to pass the time. Reading fiction and joining a book club, at the local library, to take her mind away from feeling what's buried inside her.

Walking and walking and walking—but not really for exercise. She's lost so much weight. Fifty pounds. But despite the enjoyment she gets from cooking, Charlene hasn't had a real appetite for food. Only grief.

Doesn't matter. The nights always come. Empty with want and loss. Making way for the morning and another day of pretending to be whole. Charlene had built her world around William, and when he left he took with him sacred parts of her. She wonders if she'll ever get them back. She knows that she will never forget William. But she also knows she's been grieving for too long and the pain is stopping her from moving forward.

And with Old Gabriel's death, Charlene feels like she said goodbye to someone who was more like her dad than her uncle. Since his death, she's felt lost and isolated in the bush, even though the north has always been the place she's felt most at home. Fresh air to breathe and space to move. But now it's like there is too much space. And no way to fill it up.

At Sandy's prompting, Charlene agreed to take a leave from her job and follow her sister to Regina. Too many reminders up north. Too many things keeping her frozen on the inside.

City life is foreign to Charlene. The traffic in the city. The houses that are so close to each other. The crowds of people on the street. What she is most used to is the solitude of the bush. Walking Misty helps. She takes those walks in her beaded moosehide moccasins. And, surprising to her, Charlene finds the unfamiliarity of the city gives her the space to examine her grief.

As is so often the case, her destination is Pacific Fresh Fish. It is a local business and only a few blocks from where Sandy lives and one of the only places in the city where she can find the whitefish she's used to eating. But it is another day of reflection. She chooses to take the long route through Les Sherman Park instead of a direct way down a couple of sidewalks. Through the park is a round-about way to get to the store, but one that is more scenic that's for sure. The variation will allow her to walk along meandering Wascana Creek and the willows that dot that route.

Once she and Misty arrive at the walking trail, they can barely hear the whir of city traffic. She sees a dogwood flower and for the first time in a long time it makes Charlene smile from the heart. The flower reminds her of a story from her childhood.

It was a long time ago but she remembers walking down by the river with her Kohkum Gertie. Her old grandma pointing to the blossom and saying, "That beautiful little flower reminds me of you." Kohkum goes on to describe how the dogwood is one of the only flowers that is strong and beautiful and resilient. *And determined to grow anywhere as long as it is kissed by sunshine.* Like you, she told nosisim, her granddaughter.

As Charlene muses, Misty spots a gopher ahead and tries to run after it. Stopped short though by her chain and collar. It snaps Charlene back into the present.

I have got to find something to do while in this city, she thinks to herself. She sees another small dogwood flower and hears the sound of a raven. A reminder. She needs to continue to be strong and determined to grow. *Just like Kohkum said.*

The walk to the fish store itself is effortless. A warm summer breeze is coupled with the sounds of seagulls that hang out in the city. It's soothing. She enjoys the sounds of laughter of kids playing on monkey bars and swings set up in the park.

A few minutes later, when they are back on city streets, she is greeted by lots of traffic along 13th Avenue. A market place in continuous motion. Next the welcoming sounds of chimes as she pushes open the heavy glass door to the fish store and a friendly greeting from behind the counter. No need to browse. Charlene knows exactly what she came for and heads towards the large freezer at the centre of the west wall. Two packages of white fish and fresh chowder tonight.

Although she does admit to herself that she'll be very happy in a few days. Maynard is coming to visit. And the fish he brings will be right from the lake.

32. BLESSING

"OH MY LORD! IT SMELLS HEAVENLY in here." Sandy is all smiles coming in through the bevelled-glass front door of her home. She doesn't even take the time to put her purse and keys away, her high heels announcing her arrival as she makes her way across the polished wooden floors and into the kitchen. There is some music playing—flamenco guitar. It is drowned out by conversation. "What are you cooking, Char?" Sandy lifts the lid to a pot simmering on the stainless steel stove. Her squeal of delight is accompanied by the clapping of hands as Sandy notices fresh bannock on the counter. And of course a teapot filled with wihkaskwapoy.

Charlene and Misty come in through the back screened-door. "Hungry?"

"Oh, you have outdone yourself. Wow. Is it ready?"

Charlene smiles and gestures to the patio table on the back deck. "Already set the table." The two sisters like to take their meals outdoors in the warmth of the sun.

"Busy day at work? Charlene asks.

"Well, it was busy. But a good one."

Sandy tells Charlene about the story she covered today. She still works as a television journalist and she is working on a segment featuring a benefactor who purchased an empty lot next door to a women's shelter. "The plan now is to be able to expand the play area for the kids who live there. Oh, you should see the blueprints—they're gorgeous. I'm so happy for those families. It's hard enough having to live in a shelter. But this will make the transition so much easier. I'm happy for them."

A thought suddenly crosses her mind and Sandy glances intently at her sister, and then makes a suggestion: "I hope you don't think I am out of line for suggesting this, but..." The women's shelter is within walking distance or a short cab ride from Sandy's home. She proposes that Charlene might want to give some thought to volunteering at the shelter. "Everyone can use the help of someone with a nursing background like yours. What do you say?"

Charlene says yes. It takes no time at all for the two to begin planning.

Sandy leaves the back deck and returns to the kitchen. Its ten-foot-high ceiling means she has to pull up a chair to reach what she's looking for from the top cupboard above the fridge. A city map so that she can show her sister where the shelter is located. Right beside that map is a handful of unpaid parking tickets. "Oh shit. I forgot about those." Sandy grabs them too and puts the tickets on the counter beside her purse. She reaches inside her bag to retrieve a pamphlet she picked up at the shelter earlier in the day. A few more seconds and she'll join her sister again in the backyard deck.

As she waits, Charlene smiles watching Misty play with water from the sprinkler turned on near a small herb garden. She looks towards the sun, just ever so slowly beginning to set and she whispers the words, "Thanks Kohkum. Kinanaskomitin."

33. NINA

NINA HAS LIVED MORE THAN seventy years. She has experienced more than most could handle. And today she tells the story again. The one she has told so often—of when she was a little girl. And she is required to share it again today. It is, after all, a story of healing.

It begins at a time when her friends and cousins on the Rez played a game that really did involve life and death. Pimpahta! Run! It wasn't so much a game as a way of life.

At this point in Nina's young life, it has been over sixty years since the Canadian government denied Native People the right to leave their reserve without first obtaining a pass—permission from the government. The pass system came into effect in 1885 as a way to control the movement of "rebel Indians." It came after the Red River Rebellion to ensure that farmers living in areas surrounding the reserves would be kept safe. The pass system also enabled the government to outlaw cultural practices like drumming, the sweat lodge ceremony, and smudging. It was a crime to be an Indian.

So Nina's family was relegated to an area—outdoors, but prison-like. And, each time she and her companions played in the bush, they'd sharply attune their sense of hearing. The lurking danger was not wildlife, but the probability of no life. Hearing tires rolling down bumpy grid roads meant the Indian Agent was coming. Not to bestow a pass. More likely to pluck whichever children could be rounded up from their homes and community and take them to residential school.

Even today Nina's breathing becomes rapid as she remembers and relates the trauma of watching her cousin Benny being captured.

The day was overcast, which was cause for celebration. A long stretch of hot, sunny weather had meant that the growth of meagre gardens of potatoes, corn and turnips had been stunted. Even Saskatoon berry bushes had started to prematurely ripen. Some had even dried and shrivelled. That didn't stop the kids from picking as many as they could hold though. The berries at the bottom of the tall, thick bushes were the most plump and within easy reach for small hands.

Cousin Benny had spotted a high patch that didn't get direct sunlight. The ripe berries beckoned and Benny wandered to the area nearest to the road. He was intent on claiming the prize, grunting and pulling down the thickest of the boughs. He made such a ruckus, heaving with determination and stamping on dried twigs that snapped and cracked under the weight of his feet, that he didn't hear the call.

Pimpahta!

Within moments, a big black car skids to a stop on the grid road just yards from where Benny is picking. Two white men jump out and run towards the young boy. One of those men carries a baseball bat. Nina can still see her cousin being grabbed by the hair and yanked so hard that he falls backward. There is yelling and swearing in the English language, which little Nina doesn't understand. But she knows it isn't good. Benny stands up and the one with the bat clubs him in the ribs. Blood gushes from his nose and his mouth and he cries. He falls to the ground a second time. This time the men don't wait for him to get up by himself. Each of those men grabs an arm of the small boy and stuffs him into the back of the car. They drive away.

A hysterical Nina waits in the bush, not far from where it all happened. She waits, holding her breath and saying some prayers until she can hear the tires on the road no more. Then she runs. Runs as fast as she can home.

"Kohkum! Mooshum!" she shrieks. She tells them what happened. Her grandparents' hearts sink and Mooshum sits down at the wobbly kitchen table. He knows what just happened.

Moons pass. Ohpahowipisim. August when blueberries are ready to harvest. Nocihitowipisim. September and hunting season. Pimahamowipisim. October when birds migrate. Kaskatinowipisim. November and stacking wood for winter. Thithikopiwipisim. December and the month those Indian Agents promised Benny would come home for a visit.

But that never happened.

And in Opawahcikanisis, January, that's when they took Nina too.

34. HORROR

"NINOHTI-MICISON." The frightened little Nina appeals to the nun. The girl is so famished, she forgets to say the words in English: "I am hungry." That nun gets really mad and starts herding the little girl towards the room where everyone has to go three times a day. There they are forced to their knees and have to clasp their hands. *Our Father* are the first English words Nina is cajoled into learning, often accompanied by the slap of a yardstick. But right now she's hungry and she says so again: "Ninohti-micison." I am hungry. This time the attack is brutal.

"You little heathen!" Sister St. Pancras roars. She slaps Nina across the small of her back with that yardstick. "Speak English!" she growls. Nina doesn't understand, "Ninohti-micison." The girl cries uncontrollably, her pangs of hunger even stronger than the pain of being struck. It happens again—the yardstick strikes her back. "Speak English or I'll show you what!"

"Ninohti-micison."

The nun punches Nina square on her ear and the little girl falls to the cold, marble floor. She hits her head hard, going down. The nun is enraged, "Get up! Get up now or I'll show you." Nina doesn't move, so Sister St. Pancras kicks her in the stomach. Kicks her in the buttocks. Slaps her torso hard too, not once but several times—on the abdomen and in the chest area.

"Stop it! Sister, please. She's had enough. I order you to stop!" The Mother Superior has arrived.

Little Nina wakes up in the infirmary several hours later. She doesn't speak. And then there is darkness.

Now in her seventies, when Nina retells the story, she still has to quell strong emotions. "They kept me overnight but didn't take me to the hospital even though I was throwing up blood." By the next morning, Nina had slipped into a coma. "And in that state I was, for almost a year," she tells them.

No more than five feet tall, Nina is not your typical-looking warrior. She was hired by the women's shelter as a resource for women seeking help. Elder and Cultural Liaison is her official title. But mostly, she says, she's there to help women find ways to help themselves. It's why she tells the story, "So many of us come from a place where we never should have even been. But we can find our way out."

A group of young women listen intently. Some have tears streaming down their face, understanding as Nina speaks. Hurts can be healed, but not without hope. The women sit in a circle in a large, mostly-empty room at the shelter. The smell of burning sage is thick but comforting as Sandy and Charlene enter the area. The momentary disruption of their arrival is noticed by Nina who smiles and nods, gesturing for the new visitors to join the group. Both women take a seat on the floor.

Charlene has decided that volunteering at the shelter is just what she needs. She's come here today to make introductions.

When the sharing circle comes to an end, the residents of the shelter leave for outdoor activity. As Nina packs up her bundle of sage, her rawhide rattle, and a braid of sweetgrass, the shelter's Executive Director, Marlene Perkins, enters the room.

"Thank you Nina." She tightly hugs the small-boned woman.

"I'm just happy to be here," the Old Woman replies.

"I'd like to introduce you to Charlene Bear." Marlene gestures towards Charlene. "She'll be volunteering here at the shelter. If you need her help for anything, just ask."

Charlene smiles and extends her hand in greeting.

Nina speaks. "Tanisi?" How are you, in Cree. Wondering about the name Bear and if Charlene is a speaker. Charlene feels a warmth and comfort in hearing her familiar language, which she hasn't heard since arriving in the city.

Namoha nanitaw, kitha maka?" Fine and you? The usual response. It's Nina's turn to feel happy at being fed familiarity, "Taniti ohci kitha?" Where are you from? It is so often the first question asked of someone with the same blood. The social norm in white society, "What do you do for a living?" is considered rude.

35. WOMEN'S WORK

"IT LOOKS LIKE A GREAT BIG SLAB of really, really thick rice paper. You know—the ones I use to make fresh rolls." Sandy describes her first impression of seeing a bone-dry piece of rawhide that sits atop a butcher's block in the large, industrial kitchen at the women's shelter.

"What's a fresh roll?" Her sister asks and Sandy laughs. "It's a Vietnamese dish. I keep forgetting that you don't have restaurants like this one in Deschambault. You would like fresh rolls. Very tasty. We'll pick some up on the way home."

Today is the day both Sandy and Charlene have been waiting for. Sandy has even taken the day off at the television station so she can be here for a drum-making workshop at the women's shelter. Nina is facilitating.

The workshop is being held in the shelter's kitchen, the largest room in the home. As residents continue to bring in extra tables for the project, Sandy notices the oversized sinks. There's something that looks like wet cardboard stuffed in each of them. And more of the same material is soaking in oversized bins filled with water and placed on the black-and-white tiled floor.

Drum music plays from a boom box sitting on one of the counters by the window. "Awww. Sounds awesome," Sandy says to Charlene as she begins to move her feet to the rhythm of the beat. "And listen to their voices. Beautiful voices. These women sound like angels."

Nina enters the room wearing what Sandy sees as several gigantic bracelets. The look is exaggerated because Nina is so tiny. A dozen large wooden circles are stacked on both of her arms. The rings—really big wooden bracelets—seem to Sandy an odd fashion accessory for the Elder. Nina notices Sandy's intrigue. She walks to the centre of the room and places the rings on top of a large piece of dry rawhide. "There. Almost ready." She catches Sandy's gaze, and nods. "Drum rings. Figured we need to start with an explanation of the materials we'll be using."

While the children are busy doing other activities, a group of women who live at the shelter begin filing into the kitchen. Marlene Perkins is with them, carrying a file folder as she walks directly towards the stove. She fills the kettle in preparation for making tea. Nina instructs everyone to take a spot at one of the folding tables that have been placed around the room. "But there aren't any chairs," remarks one of the residents.

Nina's response: "No. Hard to make a drum when you're sitting. But if you need one, we'll bring it over."

"Good day, ladies." Marlene is standing by the butcher's block and begins her greeting. "I want to say thank you to our Elder Nina Thomas for leading this workshop. And acknowledge some of the sponsors who've helped make it happen." She mentions organizations like the Saskatchewan Cultural Exchange Society, an organization that encourages artist projects for under-served communities, as well as the Government of Saskatchewan and the City of Regina. "We've got all afternoon for this experience. So I'll make some tea now and turn it over to Nina."

By this time, Nina has lit some sage in a shell. With her eagle feather in hand, she walks to each of the participants, instructing them to smudge. Residents are familiar with the practise. So is Sandy. But it makes Charlene a bit nervous. She whispers to Sandy, "What's she doing?" Sandy smiles, remembering the first time she took part in this form of prayer. "Smudging. The sage purifies our thoughts and prayers and actions."

It is a practicse that shouldn't be but is new to Char. Residential school and the church banned this cultural tradition, so it wasn't a part of her upbringing, especially in the north where, Sandy was surprised to learn, the church still has a foothold in discouraging cultural and spiritual ways. And, while Char has heard about smudging, she's never seen it done in person. At this moment, Char feels both uplifted, and guilty, to be taking part. She welcomes her sister's explanation, as Sandy repeats something her own teacher—Joe Bush Sr.—had told her not that long ago: "It's like when you are in church and the Catholics burn their incense at Easter time. The smoke carries your prayers up to Creator."

"I remember that scent," Charlene recalls. "You used to smudge every morning, in your room, when you came and visited us up north. And, I remember I smelled it the first time I came to this shelter. I wanted to ask you about it, but felt shy to ask, like I should already know, but didn't. I didn't want to seem ignorant. Thank you for explaining."

"I still do it every morning," Sandy explains, "but usually these days, I am outdoors on the deck. I love praying outdoors."

Next, Nina holds up a drum ring and talks about the circle. "We are all equal. No one is better. No one is worse. We are all here to learn." She asks one of the women to distribute a drum ring to each of the women, as she grabs the big piece of rawhide. It is hard and sturdy, like a piece of wood, "We'll be using this rawhide to create our drums. This is what a dried piece looks like before we begin."

Nina talks a bit about the animal that gave its life to provide the rawhide for these drums and to feed families. "All parts of the animal are used. We do not waste gifts that are given to us." She talks about how the drum is a symbol of unity and how each Nation across Canada has a drumming tradition. She tells them that each drum is unique to its own geographic area because of the animal hide from which it comes. "As an example, this is an elk hide drum." Nina sounds the instrument. "It has a big, bass sound because an elk is a very large, powerful animal." She makes the comparison by next sounding a deer hide drum. "The hide is thinner because the animal is smaller. So when it is made into a drum, the sound is smaller. Just like a deer is smaller than an elk. Similar sound, but different."

Nina motions towards what Sandy thought was wet cardboard in big bins on the floor. Nina now explains that the hide needs to be soaked for several hours, preferably overnight, before the drum-making begins. That way it can be handled and fashioned onto the drum ring. "But first we need to start cutting babiche. The rawhide strips we will use to string the drum onto the circle. Everyone head to a bin and grab a piece. There are scissors on each table."

Sandy and Charlene each do as instructed, returning to a table with their wet piece of rawhide. "It feels sticky. And it smells like cooking neckbones," Charlene jokes.

As the group of women get to work, Nina assures them that the path they have chosen in making a drum is a good one. "There are some people who say women should not drum. But I do. I figure if Creator has given me this gift of song then it is my responsibility to develop this gift and pass it on. We are among those who are called by the drum. It is something that unites us. It doesn't divide us."

Nina tells a story as the songs of the Squaw'kin Iskwewak women's drum group from Manitoba softly plays on the portable stereo.

> *Woman brought drum and song. Drum and song—a vision given to woman. Years ago, Indian people were at war amongst each other. Women would gather up the children and run deep into the bush for comfort. A woman—desperate for change amongst her village—sat for four days and nights praying to Creator for an answer. She was given the clear vision of drum*

and song. Going back to her village she would gather the people, guiding them in preparations to create the drum. Through her, heartbeat and song came. In doing this, she conveyed the Creator's message to bring peace and unity back into the hearts of the people. This is one of the many gifts woman has brought to the people.

36. FINDING MAYNARD

AS EXPECTED, IT TAKES ALL AFTERNOON to construct a drum. But when Sandy and Charlene make their way back home, they are greeted by the unexpected. Maynard's two-toned grey Dodge pick-up is parked on the street. There is no mistaking it's him. He clipped a deer on the highway last year. He wasn't hurt. The deer ran away. But the accident left the right side of his bumper with some cracks. He never got them fixed; just bandaged it up with some duct tape that has held well over the seasons. A real Indian car.

Charlene is excited to see him, "I'd recognize that Rezmobile anywhere. Maynard's here. Wasn't expecting him for another couple of days."

Once parked, she runs out on the sidewalk and goes in for a hug. "Cousin! It's so good to see you." Charlene points with her lips towards the steps leading into the house, "Astam maka, wiciwinan. Come, follow me."

Maynard smiles. "I believe I will come with you."

They make their way into Sandy's handsome home with Maynard providing commentary. "Wow, Sandy. It's really nice in here. Sure has a different feel than our little cabin, that's for sure." He takes a seat on the bench in front of the antique upright piano that Sandy recently acquired. She's been meaning to learn to play for years.

Absentmindedly pressing on a few keys, Maynard glances around and comments on a print of an Allen Sapp painting that hangs above the piano. It's an image of two work horses pulling a wooden sleigh that is being driven by an old Mooshum carrying a load of wood. "Geez, that picture reminds me of Dad," Maynard says, "except he used a snowmobile. But I do remember his stories about working with horses."

He notices a bouquet of fresh flowers and is not surprised to discover that Sandy buys flowers for herself. They brighten up the living room. The flowers are displayed on a chrome and glass coffee table next to a red leather couch. A large colourful star blanket hangs as an art piece on the north wall, catching the afternoon sunlight. The creative decoration of new and modern pieces blend in well with the old wooden floor and window sills.

Charlene has gone to the kitchen to make some tea. She asks her cousin the inevitable question once she returns to the living room: "So? You promised to bring fish. Where is it?"

"Oh yeah." Maynard excuses himself and goes out to his truck. He comes back carrying two things: a large camping cooler and a paper bag. "I brought us some dinner, ladies." He laughs. "Two all-beef patties, special sauce, lettuce, cheese, pickles, onions on a sesame seed bun. I am easily-influenced by TV commercials. Besides, sure can't get this in Deschambault."

Togetherness. Family.

Sandy feels the energy change in this little space—lighting up with happiness—as she eats her burger and watches her sister open the cooler. Char reacts with glee, as sure as a kid at Christmas. Little Misty is curious about the smell as she too awaits the opening of the package to see what's inside. The cooler is brimming with an assortment of filleted northern lake fish. Maynard's also packed a moose roast, neckbones, and steaks, and a container filled with smashed chokecherries.

Charlene holds the container close to her heart, "Oh my! Where'd you get these?"

Maynard explains that on his way through Prince Albert, he stopped in to see cousin Agnes. "She had some frozen from last season. When I said I was coming to visit with you, she insisted that I take them."

"Oh thank you, cousin. Thank you." Charlene kisses the container, "They're my favourite."

Maynard smiles. "Agnes knows that. It's why she sent them."

Sandy is curious. She has never seen smashed chokecherries before nor has she tasted them. The jar filled with them is the consistency of grainy Dijon mustard and she inquires about the taste. "Well, what can I say? It tastes like home," Charlene says. "I can teach you how to do this," she adds. "I notice a lot of chokecherry bushes growing by the creek down the road. When they're ripe, we'll go picking. But for tomorrow's dinner, I'll serve these with a side of bread pudding." She then explains that as a little girl, Agnes taught her how to smash the berries on a flat rock, mix them with lard and sugar, and then boil the mixture until it became like a pudding.

"I remember those days." Maynard becomes reflective.

Charlene returns to the kitchen to get some tea for everyone. Sandy puts on a cassette of classical music: Vivaldi's *Four Seasons*. Maynard talks about why he's arrived a couple of days early. "It's too quiet in the cabin now. Ever since Dad died."

Same reason that Charlene came to the city.

The next moments are filled with remembrances of a life well lived. Charlene tells them about the time when she hit a big rock on the grid road, which is not covered by asphalt. It put a hole in her muffler. "Holy. It was loud. Drove me crazy." The next time she'd stopped in to see Auntie Myrna and Uncle Gabriel, "Uncle asked why my car is so noisy." Charlene explained then she and Auntie Myrna went down near the river to pick some mint leaves. By the time they returned, Gabriel had already hoisted her vehicle up replaced the muffler, and changed her oil. She hadn't asked him to do it. "And he refused to take any money."

Maynard shares another story: "Remember when cousin Theo hurt his back?" Theo had a family to take care of. His small injury, slipping on fish guts, meant he'd miss the yearly hunting trip. Sustenance. Dad shot two moose that season. Dressed and packaged the meat, then delivered it to Theo's house leaving only a note. He did that on a day when he knew my cousin would be away at physiotherapy."

They finish their first pot of tea and burgers and the discussion turns to Charlene and how she's enjoying her stay in the city. "We did the most wonderful thing today, hey Sandy?" Charlene tells Maynard about the drum-making workshop and how she's grateful to have been introduced to Nina. "She doesn't make me feel inferior about things I don't know. Like smudging."

Maynard can see that the two women are excited about what they are doing. Sandy jumps in and announces, "Once the drums are dry enough—in a few days—Nina is going to teach us how to drum. And teach us some songs."

Maynard is happy to hear that Charlene seems to be finding a place of peace here in the city. He knows how much she has been suffering. "But you better not let John Wayne know you've made a drum," he says and frowns. "He'll tell you it's forbidden. Women aren't allowed."

"Ah. Did you really have to mention that name my cousin? Of all the things I am missing about the north, he is not one of them." Charlene then suggests they all take Misty for a walk. She wants to show Maynard the Wascana Creek pathway, a place that's become her friend.

37. REVENANT

THERE ARE MANY WHO WILL TELL YOU that man's most important invention is the wheel. But Nina Thomas will argue differently. She believes it is the slow cooker. It has provided years of mouth-watering aromas that feed the soul, body, and memory. As she walks into her home this evening, she revels in the the smell of great cooking and the feeling of a great sense of accomplishment, having guided a group of uncertain women towards creating their own drum. She prays most of them will now follow the traditional ways: sounding their drum and raising their voices in celebration and song.

The fragrant elk stew on the counter and the lingering scent of sage—burned at dawn—greets Nina as she enters her warm kitchen. The elk meat was a gift. The family of one of the young girls who recently left the women's shelter gave it to her. They did it as a way to thank her for ensuring their daughter was taken care of until they arrived to bring her home.

Nina sets her oversized cloth purse next to her sewing machine on the kitchen table and goes to the cupboard to retrieve a bowl. Even though there was some food and tea shared when the drum-making workshop ended, Nina purposely didn't eat too much. She knew the slow-cooked elk stew was waiting for her in her own kitchen. Next, she puts on an apron. It was also a gift, given to her by a group of students in North Central Regina, an area generally thought of as rough. But Nina knows it is also a place of rebuilding. That's why she always agrees anytime she's asked to visit and share in that part of the city. On the front of the apron is the image of a buffalo. Embroidered by hand on one of the pockets are the words: "Education is our new buffalo." Even though Nina is not preparing food, wearing her apron when she's at home is a habit, in more ways than one. Like a nun's habit that represents repentance and simplicity, Nina's apron represents preparing food: Food for the body. Food for the soul. Food for new ideas. Food as memory. Food as comfort. She's never in her kitchen without an apron.

As she ladles out a portion of the stew with an old wooden spoon that's been in the family for years, Nina ponders. Slow cooking. It's the way life should be: letting the flavours blend and simmer and compliment each other, instead of the fast-food lifestyle adopted by the new generation who never pay attention to what they are ingesting. The slow-cooking method is similar to the old ways of knowing and learning, as opposed to accepting what is being force-fed to you by someone else.

She'd like to set down her bowl on the table, but first she has to move several spools of thread, small containers of brightly-coloured beads, and bundles of ribbon out of the way. Her kitchen table is not used only for eating—it's also where she creates.

Nina hasn't always been immersed in her traditional culture. That didn't happen until after Harold, her husband, died. He passed too soon from complications due to diabetes. He had to have a leg amputated after he dropped a hammer on his toes and the injury became infected with gangrene. Broken-hearted, Nina found herself at a crossroads. Two voices had shown up. They were spirits, both promising something.

One came in a bottle. The other was the Old Voice we hear in the wind.

Her husband was gone, but their love remained. So Nina promised never to drown those memories but to keep them alive and powerful. She chose to honour his memory by embracing, learning about, and following the Old Ways. And doing this lead her to the dance.

Smudging with sage, sweetgrass, and cedar became a daily ritual—offering prayers for her children, for all children. She made a promise to Creator that she would embrace the rhythm of life no matter what it might bring. For her, it meant letting go. All of the horrible feelings associated with residential school had to fade and die. The stories could remain so that others may learn from them, but the pain had to go.

And that's when she was called by the drum. She remembers her first time dancing during the inter-tribal at a pow wow. A time when anyone and everyone is invited to dance even if you don't have an outfit. She stepped tentatively into the dance area of the pow wow arbour. At first, she simply walked in a circle along with the other dancers. It didn't take long, however, before her feet started moving to the beat. Not long after that pow wow, she pieced together her first outfit. In doing so, she resurrected the Old Traditions and the Old Ways.

Creator knows she has earned respect in her role as an Elder as she continues to beckon, influence, and encourage as many as she can back to the dance, back to the circle: a place of respect and fulfillment and pride.

As Nina finishes up the bowl of stew, she glances at a photo of her husband Harold and her thoughts make her smile. His portrait hangs on the wall above her sewing machine. On that same wall hangs an old rusted metal gate. That old rusted gate reminds Nina of the beginnings of her love for Harold.

They met at a second-hand store decades ago. Both were in their early twenties and both were looking for inexpensive dishes and towels and kitchen chairs. She was there thinking she'd find some items to decorate her first apartment, which she shared with a cousin. It was in Saskatoon's Riversdale area. Young Nina's hope was to go to university and study education, even though studying and getting a degree meant she'd have to relinquish her Indian status. She'd also have to get government approval in order to be able to study, but only if Nina was first deemed fit to be a student. The government policy of the day: the government had to decide whether she was acceptable. But her high school grades needed improvement so she decided to upgrade them in the city, find a job, and cross her fingers that she'd get accepted.

In the meantime, she worked as a cashier at Adilman's Department Store. Minimum wage in the mid-sixties was just over a dollar. That's why she was looking for bargains in the second-hand store. While browsing, she and Harold were attracted to the same small, wooden kitchen table. And attracted to each other. Harold agreed to let Nina take the table home that day, but not before she'd agreed to meet for coffee later that evening. They were together ever since, thirty years, until complications due to his diabetes took Harold to the spirit world.

That metal gate is a pivotal point in their lives together.

The gate was used to mark the entrance to Princess Alexandra School. It was in front of that gate, when it was still shiny and new, that Nina and Harold felt the magic of a first kiss. A few weeks after they'd met at the second-hand store, they'd been out for a walk and were getting ready to say goodnight. In front of the school Harold stopped walking. He looked into Nina's eyes and said, "I'm so glad we met. Hope we always stay together." And then he kissed her. She still feels the warmth of that kiss that can only come from the heart. A bonding kissed with magic, and the forging of a promise that would never be broken.

Nina wipes away a tear. She was happy to have been able to bring that gate home. She'd found it earlier in the spring when she was visiting Saskatoon and going down memory lane. As she drove past the old school she noticed the main building was being renovated. She saw the now-rusted gate laying in a heap of rubble destined for the dump. Nina stopped her car, opened her trunk, and took the gate home that very day, along with its associated warm memories. It's a comfort to her that the gate now hangs on her wall. Something tangible and sacred that represents a piece of her life with Harold.

38. MESSENGER

FINDING BALANCE IS AN UNENDING QUEST and dance unto itself. Nina knows this. She also knows the days pass too quickly. Gone before you even realize. It's the reason she's already made plans for tomorrow. She'll conduct another sharing circle at the shelter. Each woman who takes part can talk about whatever is on her mind. Nina knows her discussion will be about the Medicine Wheel.

She knows that so many young Aboriginal people have never heard about the teachings of mental, spiritual, emotional, and physical enlightenment. She will share her thoughts on walking the earth in a good and peaceful way, and why it is important to connect with spirit. And she has some tools.

Nina has beaded on a large piece of soft, white leather an image of the Medicine Wheel. The four colours are divided into four equal parts. Red, black, yellow, and white—representating each colour of the human race. She packs the leather reminder in a bag along with a list of books and places it all beside her purse on the kitchen table. This way when she leaves in the morning there is no way to forget. That happens sometimes. Leaving the house without essential items. Not sure if the forgetfulness comes with age or just being so busy.

Nina decides that she'll talk about the Medicine Wheel and why it's important to have this knowledge before she begins to teach the women at the shelter how to make an outfit for those who wish to do so. She wants them to dance too. Maybe follow their own path of enlightenment. Thoughts about the next day bring a feeling of accomplishment and Nina smiles at herself in the mirror in the bathroom before removing her dentures and combing her long grey hair. She'll braid it again in the morning.

It's been a good day. What she's done means women will drum. What she plans to do means women will dance. She says a silent prayer before moving back the handmade star blanket on her bed , another gift, this one from her students at the university. It is time for some rest. She closes her eyes and sleep takes her immediately.

He comes during the night on hind legs as strong and sturdy as an oak tree. Nina is standing in a clearing in the bush. She hears him before she sees him. But there is no fear.

Tanisi i-isithihkasoyin? The creature asks for her name. She tells him.

Kaskiti Maskwas Iskwiw, her spirit name: Black Bear Woman.

The wind in the forest stops. The moon illuminates the spot on which she is standing as brightly as a headlamp.

The creature seems as tall as the trees. He dons the antlers of an elk but his face is human. It is a kind face. The creature snorts and paws at the ground, sending up swirls of dust. He's come to give Kaskiti Maskwas Iskwiw a warning.

> *Ravens are old and cunning and wise,*
> *stealing when the sun is high.*
> *They do not fly at night.*
> *If you see this turn back.*
> *Why?*
> *Raven foreshadows doom in black sky.*
> *Listen,*
> *ravens do not fly at night.*

39. NEWLY ARRIVED

IT IS ALMOST MIDNIGHT. A frantic knocking at the door to the women's shelter late at night signals one of two scenarios. Someone is in dire need of help. Or someone is very drunk and confused. It is for both of these reasons there is no such thing as a skeleton staff at the shelter no matter the time of day or night.

The doorbell at the residence rings loudly three times. Whoever is outside begins to pound on the door again. Three staff members from various parts of the building converge at the entrance. Another stands by the telephone in the foyer, in case 9-1-1 needs to dialed.

"Hello? Who's there?"

"I need help." It's a woman's voice.

"Are you alone?"

"Yes. Please let me in."

One of the night staff turns on the exterior light and opens a small viewing window on the heavy wooden door. She sees a young Native woman in obvious distress. She's alone. Her left eye is bruised, the eyelid almost swollen shut. There is a cut on her top lip.

The staff member who's holding the telephone is told there will be no need to call the police. There is no trouble at the doorstep. Only someone in need of help. "She likely needs a medical kit. Go get it and some ice. Both are in the kitchen!"

The front door is unlocked and the young woman is escorted inside. Her injuries are not life-threatening but it's clear the woman is traumatized. She can't fully explain how she came to be at the steps to the shelter at this time of night. She seems disoriented although there is no indication of intoxication or the effects of narcotics, details the staff has been trained to look for. The woman says she is cold. She is given a blanket and guided to the kitchen where a pot of herbal tea is ever-present and ready for use. "Would you like some ice for your eye?"

"No. I just want to sit down." The woman begins to sob.

Someone hands her a tissue. "It's okay. You'll be safe now." Everyone waits several minutes before forms are taken from a desk in the main office and the questions begin.

The woman says she woke up on the floor of a cabin where she's been staying. Up north. That was yesterday morning. She was alone when she woke up.

She says she doesn't remember calling anyone nor does she know how she got to the city. "It feels like I have been travelling all day. But how can I not remember?" She begins crying again. Blows her nose. Regains her composure and continues to fight with her memory.

She says she vaguely remembers cooking some food. Last night. It was quiet in the cabin except for the television that was on but turned down low. "I remember now. It was just starting to get dark."

She says her companion came home late and she was upset that he didn't call to let her know he'd be late. "He was sitting on a chair by the front door and after he took off one of his steel-toed work boots he threw it at me. It's all I remember."

"Don't push yourself right now. We can talk again in the morning. You should get some sleep first. You'll have to make a statement to police. But that can wait until daylight too."

The woman didn't have any luggage with her when she arrived at the shelter, but she did have a purse.

"Do you have an identification with you? Health card?

Driver's license? We're going to need your name before we can allow you to stay the night."

"Oh. Yes. I have that right here." The young woman grimaces as she digs through her hand bag.

"Thank you. And please, no more worries, you are safe here."

A staff member named Nickita checks the young woman's ID and nods her head. "You will be safe here now, Mary Ann."

40. THE DEN AGAIN

IT HAS BEEN A LONG TIME since Sandy's been at this sleazy cowboy bar known as The Den in downtown Regina. It's a downtown club with a dubious reputation. Every city has one and Sandy knows anything goes here pretty much every night.

Like the last time she visited. Sandy can't understand how she managed to get talked into patronizing the place again. But here she stands, with her sister and her cousin, secretly hoping none of them get stabbed. It can be that type of place.

She notices the drug dealers as soon as they enter The Den. These shifty-eyed demons try to remain inconspicuous, waiting in darkened corners until someone gives them a look or a nod. If someone does acquiesce, next is a trip to the washroom. It doesn't take much imagination to know what they are doing.

The décor of this place hasn't changed. Each table is still covered with a terrycloth topper with an elastic bottom that quickly snaps off and is washed at the end of each night. The place still has a pronounced smell of stale cigarette smoke and spilled beer. And the clientele continues to be an eclectic mix of people. Maynard insisted they all come here tonight. Sandy decided to indulge her cousin's apparent lust for danger, even though she tried to talk everyone into going to a quiet wine bar just down the street from where she lives.

The thing is Sandy no longer drinks. Neither does Charlene. Maynard is known to nurse a beer or two but hardly ever. Wihkaskwapoy is his drink of choice and it suits him. But he says he wants to hear live music. And since the disco era, finding a live band is no longer the norm. So The Den it is tonight.

It all started because Charlene brought up the subject of how much she misses the fiddle dance. Up north, there is always one held in the winter season, sometimes more than one. Even more are held during the summer months. When Maynard mentions there's one scheduled in Pelican Narrows at the end of the month the memories pour out. Mostly because neither Sandy nor Charlene are likely to be there at the end of next month. They are in the city now.

Still, Charlene talks about "Whiskey Before Breakfast" and "The Flop-eared Mule." They were Uncle Gabriel's favourite old fiddle tunes. How Char misses him. He was her first dance teacher She smiles at the memory.

"Well, certainly someone will be flop-eared here before the end of the night," Sandy makes the joke as they take a seat at a small table near a jukebox. There is no other place to sit. The Den is packed but the dance floor is quiet for now. The band has taken a break. Charlene glances around and to her delight she spots a sign. It says tonight is polka night so there will be a fiddle player on stage after all. Once she stops grumbling, Sandy notices that mixed in with the usual crowd there are several older couples here tonight, and they look happy. "Maybe the night won't be so bad," she concedes to herself.

"This place doesn't seem so bad," Charlene says. She decides she will order a diet coke as she glances around the room.

Sandy is inclined to agree. "It seems okay tonight, I guess. It certainly is an interesting place. Rumour has it that if you head out to the alley, there is a secret entrance to a gay club. A place called The Back Door. But I've never seen it. Years ago, I went back there once to check it out. But all I saw were garbage cans and an empty parking lot for the office tower next to this building."

"Oh, it's not a rumour honey," the waitress pipes up upon overhearing Sandy's comment. "You must have checked on a night when that club was closed. For members only. They aren't open all the time." The waitress then turns her attention to Maynard, "And for you honey? What can I bring you?" He orders a club soda. "Yep. Club soda it is then. Guess I won't be expecting a big tip from this table tonight."

"What's that supposed to mean?" Charlene says indignantly.

"Oh, who knows?" Sandy replies. "If you look around, there are no brown faces other than ours. Maybe our waitress is just one of those people."

The indifference shown by the waitress is not something Charlene is used to. Up north the faces she sees are brown faces more often than any other. For her, confronting racism as an Aboriginal woman, even in its mildest form, is not an everyday occurrence. Definitely not something she is used to. And she doesn't like it. Charlene is not sure how to feel or react but something happens that causes another reaction: excitement when she spots a man with a fiddle. It's Brian Sklar with his Prairie Fire Band. At least, that's what's written on the poster hanging next to the stage. The fiddler is tall and thin with a dark handlebar moustache.

Charlene's eyes follow him as he walks to the stage. "Sandy. I have an idea. Excuse me for a sec." She approaches the musician and whispers something in his ear. She comes back to the small table grinning from ear to ear. "Maynard, get your shoes on! It's time for some jigging."

Next, the fiddle player walks up to the microphone and announces: "Ladies and Gentlemen. Welcome back. Now, I know it's polka night here at the old Den but tonight we have a special surprise. All the way from northern Saskatchewan, the champion jiggers of last winter's Voyageur Winter Festival in Winnipeg." He motions for Charlene and Maynard to take to the dance floor. "Charlene and Maynard Bear are here to show you some fast and fancy moves with this tune we call ...."

Because Charlene has been wearing her moccasins, pretty much since the day she's arrived in the city, she is wearing something comfortable for dancing. Maynard isn't sure about the tobacco-coloured cowboy boots he's wearing. But they'll have to do. All eyes are on the cousins as they line up in front of the stage. Men and women—most of whom look to be in their sixties—smile and clap, waiting to see jigging. It is an instant hit. A style of dance not often performed in a country bar in the middle of the city nor in the south of the province at all for that matter. All Sandy can do is smile.

The squirrel of the bagpipes. Yes. Sandy knows the word is "skirl" but "squirrel" sounds funnier. It's what she thinks of when the fiddle sounds the first note indicating that the time has come to strike up the band.

Sandy is delighted to watch her sister and her cousin move in precise time with each stroke of the fiddle. The Red River Jig and its intense pace. They move with such grace and joy it's as though the music is a part of their DNA. It makes Sandy feel like crying but she's too busy smiling and laughing out loud. For a moment it reminds her of how at peace she is, and how whole she feels, when pow wow dancing. The traditional dances are very public celebrations of culture and love. She is happy that jigging provides the same feelings for Charlene and Maynard.

Suddenly this damp, dark nightclub sparks a memory. Sandy unexpectedly thinks about John Wayne. Why? Maybe it's the place itself. Do the walls tell stories? Sandy remembers a tall, chisel-jawed Native man making eye contact with her here the first time she visited The Den. It was a couple of years ago. She recalls watching him as he bought himself a drink and then ordered an extra double-vodka. He was carrying the drinks over to where she had been sitting but stopped when another handsome man sat beside her first and offered a shooter. Could that have been John, carrying that double vodka that was meant for her? The thought is fleeting.

She shakes her head and her pondering comes to an abrupt stop, replaced by elation as that first song ends and the crowd yells for more. It's a respite and looks like the musician is enjoying the change in pace. The fiddle player again tucks his instrument under his chin and the reel "Drops of Brandy" begins. Charlene and Maynard move and laugh and jig. Sandy is ecstatic, knowing the crowd is embracing a part of her culture and her family's culture. And they keep shouting for more.

41. WHAT THE HELL?

BECAUSE IT IS MIDNIGHT—merry times and reveille aside—it's time to go home. Sandy's back at the TV station in the morning. Charlene volunteers at the women's shelter in the afternoon. Besides, it's late. And time to go. The evening out didn't cost anyone a dime. Once Charlene and Maynard started jigging people paid for their drinks. May have been easier to do because they only had sodas.

But at some point during the night something changed. Someone started sending Maynard slippery nipple cocktails and Pilsner beer. Because it's the worst kind of alcohol—free—he accepts. More than once.

As hours advance, the women make their case. "Time to head home, cousin." But then the benefactor of the suds arrives. It's the young Shad Nielsen who offered Maynard and his dad sandwiches in the ice shack months ago. He is of drinking age now and sporting a tan that lingers from his recent trip to the Caribbean. Who knew that sandwich sales could be so lucrative?

"Hey. Saw you out there and I remembered. You're from Deschambault." He turns his attention to Sandy and Charlene, "Don't remember seeing you there, but hello. Great dancing." Meant, of course, for Charlene.

The remainder of the evening is filled with fishing stories and talks of ice and cold, and trying to find some warmth on the frozen lake. Neither Sandy nor Charlene protest when

Maynard suggests he'll stay a while, visit with Shad, and take a cab home later.

"Well that Shad sure seems like a nice young man, don't you think, Sandy?" Charlene asks while waiting for the light to turn green at the corner of Albert Street and 13th Avenue.

"He's a doll, I'm sure. But what's up with you?" Sandy says, "Holy, you are such a good dancer. So happy we went out tonight. That place wouldn't have been my first choice but now I am happy we went there. Awww. You looked so radiant and happy. You made me smile." Sandy places her hand over her heart.

Because there is a full moon that will rise in the next couple of nights it's not even dark when the sisters arrive back home. Obviously street lamps provide illumination, but they wouldn't be necessary on a night like tonight. Charlene feels it's as if Grandmother Moon is giving them her blessing. She decides that she's made the right decision to spend some time in the city away from old memories up north, and spending time getting to know her sister, Sandy, better. It is quiet when they pull up on the street in front of the character home. No rush of traffic like during the day. Although both women are a bit startled at hearing the sound of a raven. *Squawk!*

"That's odd," says Sandy. "I always thought that birds bunked down for the night, except for owls of course. I wonder what he's doing up at this hour?"

"Must be the moon," Charlene responds. "It's so bright maybe he thinks it's daytime." She snickers and offers to unlock the door. On the other side of the door, Misty is yelping with joy that her best friends have come home.

"Come on, girl," Sandy pets the dog on the head. Misty bolts out as soon as the door opens. "Time for one more pee before bedtime." While Sandy stays with her pup out on the front lawn, Charlene notices the red light flashing on the answering machine. There's a message. She hits play.

"Hi. This is a message for Charlene. It's Nickita over at the shelter. Listen, I checked the schedule and know that you aren't due to come in until tomorrow afternoon. But we are wondering if you might be able to make it in just after breakfast tomorrow? A new client showed up on our doorstep tonight. She seems disoriented and has some bruising on her face and upper body. And she says she doesn't want to go to the hospital to get checked over tomorrow." Slight pause. "Because you are a nurse, I'm hoping you won't mind taking a look at her injuries and maybe talk with her? She says she came from up north. Maybe you know her? Anyhow, have a nice evening. And if you are able to come in early, that would be great. Thanks."

42. MAKING SENSE

MAYNARD WAS QUIET AS A MOUSE coming home last night. Even Misty didn't signal his arrival with her usual frolicking and barking that would have woken up everyone in the house.

He is asleep on the couch, covered up by a colourful star blanket that Sandy bought from one of the vendors at a Round Dance during her first year of learning.

Sandy goes out of her way to remain as quiet as possible so as not to disturb him. As she heads into the kitchen she notices that Maynard has set the coffee for her. He's left a note saying: *Good morning, Cousin. Coffee is ready and I have cut up some fruit for you. It's in the fridge. Took some bread out of the freezer so you can have toast too. Enjoy your day.*

Awww, what a sweetie, she thinks. Someday he'll make someone a very good wife.

As the coffee brews, Sandy thinks about what she'll wear to work today. And she finds herself hoping that Charlene will cook those neckbones that Maynard brought with him. Moose neckbones with boiled potatoes and onions. The meat on a neckbone is soft and flavourful. It flakes off on your fork with a subtle taste that says wild and free. And your fingers always end up getting messy.

Her thoughts are interrupted by Misty pawing at the back door and Charlene walking down the stairs and entering the kitchen. "Up early," Sandy observes. "Coffee's almost ready."

"Hi, my beautiful sister. Hey? Who let the dog out?" Sandy opens the screen door to let her pup in.

"Must have been Maynard. You know, I've just had the best sleep that I've had in ages. So much fun to dance last night. But, I am a little stiff. Must be getting old."

Charlene then tells Sandy about the message on the answering machine. "I would like to help out. So of course I will go in early," she says. "While I am really enjoying my volunteer work at the shelter, I just can't believe that there are still men out there who treat women so badly." She tells Sandy that the new client Nickita mentioned is from up north. "Wonder if I know her?"

An hour later Charlene stands in the kitchen of the shelter, where the troubled young woman filled out some forms hours earlier. Nina is there too.

"Do you want me to come with you? When you meet Mary Ann? Staff says she isn't saying much. But whatever happened to her, she needs to know it wasn't her fault."

Nickita is still on shift and presents Mary Ann to Charlene and Nina.

"Oh my God. Sister," Charlene recognizes her immediately. "Oh my God. What happened?"

43. WARTS

M ARY ANN BURSTS INTO TEARS, mostly grateful tears to see a familiar face. Charlene gives her a hug and it causes a wince. "Oh, not so hard, Char." Mary Ann wipes her nose with the sleeve of her shirt, and adds, "There seems to be some bruising along my ribs."

"Oh my sister. What happened?" Charlene is shaking her head, and holding Mary Ann's tiny hands between her own.

Charlene then turns toward Nina. "Mary Ann, I'd like to introduce you to Nina. She's our Elder and advisor here at the shelter. Sometimes all we seem to need is for someone to show us the pathway. Happiness lies within. With prayer and meditation, you may be able to find it. Nina can help you. We will all help you. But, can you tell us how you got here?"

"I don't know!" Mary Ann crumbles and covers her face with both hands.

"That's okay and not important right now. We are all just glad you are somewhere safe," Charlene says, silently cursing her cousin. She is certain John Wayne has something to do with this situation.

Once Mary Ann regains some composure, Nina smiles gently at her, knowing her hurt. She has seen it so many times before. She's felt it too. And, she has found her way out. Her life's goal now is to help others do the same: find a way to move on.

"But how is this possible?" Mary Ann seems confused at

being at a women's shelter in Regina, so far away from De-schambault. She's also confused to be introduced to a small elderly woman who has been introduced as an Elder. "John has always told me that women are forbidden from leading ceremony. We aren't leaders. He says we're unpure. He told me only men are allowed to conduct ceremony. That's the way it's always been done."

Nina smiles ruefully at this. "Oh my child. I'm sorry someone told you that." She holds Mary Ann's hand in gentle reassurance and begins telling a story. It starts with the words, "What you say reminds me of when my husband Harold was still alive...." Nina's face lights up at the quirky memory.

It had to do with how to properly bake a ham. The Old Woman says she and her husband rarely disagreed, except for that ham. Ever since she could remember, Nina would cut the roast in two, then baste before setting it in the oven to slowly and succulently cook. Until one day Harold questioned her: "You don't have to cut it, you know. It'll still bake and taste just as good."

His words are battle territory. The kitchen. Her territory, which Nina feels a need to defend. "No, it needs to be cut in two."

"Why?"

"Because that's the way it's always been done in my family."

"Yes, but why?" Harold insists.

His wondering causes the young bride to question it herself and sent her to the phone to call her mom. "Mom, why do we cut a ham in two before baking?"

"Well dear, that's the way it's always been done. Your Kohkum cut the roast, and now so do I, and, of course, so do you. It's been that way for years."

Not a good enough explanation for this battle. So, Nina decides another call is in order to solve this dilemma. She dials her Kohkum. "Oh Nosisim, so good to hear from you!" her granny is happy to hear from her granddaughter. "Oh? Yes,

I used to cut my roast in two until I bought a bigger roasting pan at a garage sale."

"That's the reason you cut it in two?"

"Well of course, my girl. A large ham doesn't fit in a small roasting pan unless it's cut in two."

The story causes everyone to laugh, especially Nina, who brings the conversation back to the present. "And that's why we need to question some things. Just because someone tells you, that's the way it's always been done doesn't mean there isn't room for change or growth. Or doing things another way. A way that feels right to you."

Mary Ann has giggled so hard, she needs to reach for a tissue to wipe her nose and dry her eyes. A much needed respite from her broken heart. Nina offers her more reassurance. "And, there is nothing unpure about a woman," Nina says. "We give life. We save lives. We support each other."

Mary Ann begins to cry. A soft sobbing, as if she is letting out decades of pain that live inside her just under the surface of her skin.

"We need to smudge," Nina suggests and begins to remove items from the bag she is carrying. She pulls out a pouch made with red felt. Inside there is tobacco. When she also removes a bong neither Charlene nor Mary Ann are sure how to react. They want to laugh but will not. It's clear the device—used for smoking cannabis or hashish—has been damaged. The spout where someone would inhale the essence of burning drugs has been broken off, leaving a hole in the bong. It's where Nina places some sage. "I found this in the basement this morning. My son left it last time he visited. Strange looking thing. So, I called him and asked him what it is and he told me it is a smudge pot. It works great. The smoke travels up. I just wonder why I have never seen one before? It seems more efficient than a shell."

Bong aside, the women quell their desire to snicker. They elect not to explain to Nina what a bong is generally used for and they smudge, cascading the healing smoke over their heads, heart, and body. Mary Ann knows how to do this because John Wayne has shown her. To Charlene it is new and recently welcomed. Because of Sandy's explanation, and Nina's teachings, Char no longer feels that smudging to offer prayer is forbidden. They all pray for goodness, for acceptance, and for healing. Until the time comes for the reason Charlene came in early today. It is time to do her job.

"I need to check you out, Mary Ann."

The cautious young woman removes her blouse and pants. As Charlene slowly checks different parts of Mary Ann's body, she asks whether certain bruises still hurt.

"Yes, of course. But I still don't remember how these got here."

"We need to see if you were raped." Charlene knows it's sensitive to suggest an internal examination but it is procedure. And Mary Ann is still adamant that she will not go to hospital.

"Raped? I loved him. How could rape even be a part of that?" Mary Ann wipes away another onslaught of tears. But she does what she is asked, and lays on the soft couch in the common room, opening her legs for Charlene to take a look. It is understood that the closed French doors are off limits to every other staff or resident during these moments. Some things are unspoken but everybody knows.

"Oh my, Mary Ann. You have warts. Genital warts that might someday mess with your reproductive health. How long have these been here?"

"What? Oh my God. I got checked just after meeting John six months ago, and I didn't have anything."

So, what's John Wayne been up to in those six months? Obviously no good, and obviously with someone infected with warts. And it wasn't Mary Ann.

Charlene says nothing but she is disgusted. She suspects it was John Wayne who gave Mary Ann not only these warts, but her bruises and memory loss, too. And, if she had little regard for her cousin before she has even less now.

44. PREPARING FOR A SHIFT

IT HAS BEEN MORE THAN A WEEK and since arriving at the shelter, Mary Ann's middle name has been numbness. She refuses to eat. Shelter staff have been bringing her crackers with thick slices of marble cheddar and fresh fruit. This morning, Charlene even offers wild blueberries from home, another gift which made its way south when Maynard arrived for his visit. But even the familiarity of sweet berries doesn't prompt Mary Ann to eat. Instead, it is a sad song from her wounded heart that fills the room as she turns to the opposite side of the bed, closes her eyes, and remains silent when Charlene offers the food. There are no tears from Mary Ann anymore, only heavy sighs as she continues to weep silently on the inside.

Charlene covers her with a light sheet, leaving the multigrain crackers and a glass of water on the bedside table but taking the cheese and fruit from the tray. Charlene knows her pain. Different but similar. Pain is pain and needs to be felt, honoured, and acknowledged. She knows because she has lived through similar deep pain. Charlene takes the fresh food with her after Mary Ann refuses to eat because she doesn't see any sense in letting the fresh items spoil. *It is a sin to waste food.* Charlene can still hear her Kohkum saying that. As she quietly closes the door, she notices Nina sitting on a soft, light purple wingback chair in the large upstairs corridor. The chair is placed beside a large window that lets in the light and a view of a leafy elm. The old tree blocks the view of traffic and the busy street below. Its trunk has been banded in an effort to prevent tent caterpillars from further infestation and causing even more destruction. Fitting, Nina thinks, as she ponders the healing road ahead for the young woman who refuses to eat and to get out of bed.

"I am starting to worry," Charlene whispers.

"Don't," Nina replies. "She is grieving and acknowledging her pain. I know too many people who never honour their pain. They carry on like nothing has happened and pretend that everything is okay and it eventually bites them in the ass. They might develop stomach problems or heart palpitations. Or they turn to addictions. Their pain turns into disease because they refuse to acknowledge the darkness within them." Charlene steps in closer to hear and as she does Nina takes the small bowl of blueberries from the tray. "Haven't had these in a while." She smiles and she slowly pops each small berry into her mouth, remembering her own happy times picking berries for her family. Nina continues to speak. "It's only after Mary Ann feels her pain that she'll be able to let it go and move on. I've been praying for her. She's going to be all right. It's why she ended up here. We are going to help her."

The two women slowly make their way down the grand wooden staircase. When they reach the bottom, Nina suggests that Mary Ann join them tonight. "It's a Full Moon Ceremony. You have any more berries at home?"

Charlene tells Nina that she's never been to such a ceremony, "What'll we do?"

"We pray and we sing," says Nina. The old woman explains that the prayers offered are mostly prayers of gratitude. The songs are songs of joy. She asks Charlene to call Sandy and invite her as well. "I need the two of you to help me get ready. You need to collect wood because we'll offer food to the fire to feed the spirits. It's why I asked about the berries. We will sing to our Grandmother Moon and ask for guidance. But mostly, it's a time to rejoice in being a woman. That girl upstairs needs to be with us."

Nina describes a place not far from the city. It's called Kinook-imaw alongside the Town of Regina Beach. There is a bluff that overlooks Last Mountain Lake, or Long Lake, which is what the Ancestors called the area. Kinookimaw. It is historically significant land and a place where Aboriginal people used to hunt, fish, camp, and pick berries and medicines. Fields of wild sage still grow in abundance and rat root and sweetgrass can be found by the willows near the ponds that dot the landscape. Nina says she's been visiting the area all her life, "We used to dance there. Now too many people have built houses. I still go picking there though." She pauses and glances with thoughtful expression towards the front door. "Some say the Big Ones still live out there and show themselves to those in need of answers. Or those in need of a lesson."

Charlene interrupts, not quite following. "Who shows themselves?"

"The sasquatch. Or whatever you choose to call him. Spirit beings who have always protected the land and those who pray for balance. Some call him Bigfoot. Some call him Bush Man. He's a shape-shifter."

Nina laughs and talks about a documentary she watched on television the previous night. A group of people had assembled and described their adventures camping in remote areas and carrying special equipment. "They were trying to capture a Big One or at least take a photo. But it'll never happen. You can't capture a spirit. That's what the Big Ones are."

Charlene's squirms upon hearing this story. A crease develops between her brows and the corners of her mouth turn slightly downward. Nina notices her fear and pauses to reassure her. "And, yes, they are likely to be watching us tonight when we are out on the land but no need to be concerned. They've been watching you for years, my girl, in one form or another. They are always around. I've heard some people describe them as

what they call a giant." She stops for a moment. "When I was
a girl, Kohkum used to talk about this Spirit being having long
legs and a long face, like a horse. She told me she had seen him.
And, I've heard stories about the elusive one having horns like
an elk or moose. Like I said, a shape-shifter. No one can ever
really explain these sightings for sure. You just know when
the Big One is present. But no need for you to ever worry. I
have always heard the Elders say that so long as your heart is
pure, and you do right, their role is to protect. "

"You ever see one?" Charlene asks, aching to know.

"I haven't actually seen one but I know they are there."
Nina winks.

"How?"

Nina explains that there are ways of knowing without seeing. She talks about when she is picking berries on the land
in Kinookimaw and she feels like she's being watched, but
when she turns to look, there is no one there. She talks about
saying prayers in the wind and making an offering of tobacco
to Mother Earth, and then seeing movement in her periph-
eral vision. But when she looks more closely, there is no one
there. She talks about when she goes for walks along the quiet
Kinookimaw pathway by the lake and she hears a twig snap
behind her, she turns to look, but there is no one there. She
talks about familiar smells when sitting out near the lake: the
fragrance of wild flowers in bloom. The scent of new growth
and sap on the trees. A whiff of wet freedom and wonder as
algae stretches up along the shoreline. And then something
she cannot place? Like a pheromone, recognized only by the
most primal of senses. She surveys the area trying to identify
the source, but when she looks, there is no one there.

45. GRANDMOTHER MOON

A BIG BONFIRE IS ALREADY ROARING as Sandy, Charlene and, yes, Mary Ann drive up near the spot where the Moon Ceremony is set to happen. Atop a strikingly beautiful bluff that provides a perfect view of the lake and surrounding landscape. Char and Sandy had collected and stacked the wood earlier in the afternoon as Nina requested. Now, the sparks fly, heralding the praise they will offer within minutes.

"You have skirts?" Nina smiles upon seeing her friends arriving wearing jeans.

"Oh my God. No. Didn't know there was a dress code." Sandy feels sheepish in reply. She should have known to wear a skirt. Something Joe and Amos had taught her a couple of years ago. But the busyness of the day caused her to rush and forget. Ribbon skirts are considered sacred, a symbol of resilience and survival, because they touch the ground and connect to spirit.

"It's okay," Nina assures them. "I've been sewing for weeks now. There are several in the back of my van. Go and pick one."

The jean-clad trio open the hatch to Nina's old, rusted van (which has seen many miles and provoked even more smiles). They find several of the most elaborately ribbon-designed skirts. Sandy looks at the skirt and thinks they are beautiful. She chooses one that is made of a bright yellow fabric and decorated with purple, red, blue, and pink ribbons. The sound of an owl hoots incessantly once she makes her choice. Charlene chooses a purple skirt with blue, yellow, and white ribbons. When Mary Ann chooses her skirt, sky blue with gold, yellow, white and grey ribbons, she hears a raven cawing and flying overhead. She admires the skirt, thinking it odd to be hearing the sound of birds that should be sleeping for the night.

Finally, and at Charlene's prompting, Mary Ann reluctantly agreed to get out of her bed at the shelter and join the ceremony. Now, she is glad she came. She knows the night air, full moon, and the company of Charlene, Sandy, and Nina will be good medicine for her. Mary Ann admits that she's been spending too much time alone. Always has. And, too much time alone with only your own thoughts as company can be hazardous. But since arriving at the shelter, Mary Ann has felt safe. These three women have made sure of it. She thinks their friendship may be the answer to her lifetime of prayers. And, she decides, it is those prayers of gratitude that she will offer tonight. Grandmother Moon, the land, and this fire as her witnesses and carrying her prayers.

"This is stunning!" Sandy exclaims, pulling the colourful skirt over the jeans she's wearing. She asks about the significance of the ribbon skirt design.

Nina promises to explain later. "I want to have a workshop at the shelter and teach everyone how to make them," she smiles, "but for now, we have some singing to do."

She hands Sandy and Charlene each a hand drum. Instruments that have never been sounded. Nina was gifted with them last month but wanted to wait until a Full Moon Ceremony. Tonight is that night. The drums that were made at the shelter workshop earlier in the week are still not dry enough to be used. So the gifted drums are the ones that are supposed to be here tonight. They come from a family who lost a loved one a year ago to the day. An acknowledgement of their daughter walking this Earth and leaving behind things upon which to build. So these drums are the ones that will sound. And remember.

The three women follow the Elder to a circle of people waiting by the fire. Sandy recognizes only a couple of faces but nods to all those present. Nina places a large amount of dried sage in a familiar shell, having left the bong at home tonight. She closes her eyes as the smoke begins to drift skyward. She begins to chant a sweet melody that is filled with warmth.

"Sisters, welcome." Nina hands the smudge bowl to Sandy and indicates by making a gesture with her hand that Sandy is to offer all present a chance to smudge and begin their prayers. First by cleansing the spirit with the smoke from the burning sage. Nina describes the purpose of the ceremony: to offer gratitude. As she continues to speak and sing and offer prayers, Sandy is certain that tonight's Full Moon is rising faster than she normally sees it ascend. The sound of a crackling fire provides ambience and a sense of serenity. For the first time all week, the wild Saskatchewan wind has slowed to a gentle and barely-present breeze this night. For this, Sandy finds herself offering gratitude. Next, she isn't sure if her eyes are playing tricks on her but she swears there are images of people dancing within the flames. She rubs her eyes. Looks again. The images are gone.

Next, as Sandy holds up her palms skyward offering prayer, she swears that an unseen entity is reaching out to her. It is the strangest sensation. The skin on her hands goes cold, as though handling a bag of ice. Next, she feels encircled by a phantom gust of wind that seems to pay attention to her alone. Startled, she opens her eyes, which were previously closed in respectful meditation.

Again, she sees the fire flare. Flames jump up six feet from the bed of glowing coals, which keep the fire pit ignited. But no other person flinches. No one seems to notice that the flames have flared almost uncontrollably. They remain at peace and in prayer. Except for one.

Just then, Mary Ann approaches Sandy and whispers in her ear. "You won't believe this. I have just been shit on by a bird.

Right on my forehead. What's that supposed to mean?"

"Maybe it means your luck is changing, Mary Ann. Maybe it's a signal that it's time to wipe away what's been holding you back," Sandy whispers back, wondering where the wisdom of her words came from.

Maybe the fire.

46. WHEN WORLDS COLLIDE

First thing next morning, Sandy awakens to the smell of fresh coffee brewing and the sounds of someone moving around in the kitchen. She grabs her colourful housecoat and slips into it. The fabric is a soft silk with a butterfly motif.

"Well, good morning," she smiles at Maynard, "someone's busy today. What's up lamb chop?" It isn't small talk. Sandy is genuinely interested, watching Maynard packing what looks to be a picnic lunch.

"Hey, cuz." Maynard fetches a mug from the cupboard. "Seeing how y'all had a girls' night last night, I thought I'd head out of the city for the day. We'll take Misty too."

"We?"

That's when Maynard explains that he's been feeling out of place, not being used to the pace of this city. "But don't get me wrong. I love your home. Just feel the need to explore the land a bit. You remember Shad?"

"Oh, yes, that nice young man from The Den."

Maynard tells her Shad has invited him for a long hike in the Condie area. It is a nature refuge just north of Regina with walking trails, a small lake stocked with trout, and a picnic area. "Heck, maybe we'll even do some fishing." That statement makes Charlene giggle, knowing there is nothing that can rival northern lake fish. She's quietly entered the kitchen from the back deck where she's already enjoyed her second cup of Maynard's brew.

"Fair enough. Sounds like a nice day in store for you May-nard. Think you'll be home for dinner? I can throw some chops on the barbecue."

Maynard smiles and agrees to cook dinner once he's home later in the day. "I've been watching the cooking channel too," he smiles. "Saw a recipe for pulled pork and another for baked beans. I think it's what's supposed to be on your plate and in your tummies later tonight."

"Holy!" Sandy exclaims and raises her mug of coffee. "Sounds like a plan. I am in." A car horn beeping on the street outside Sandy's home lets them know Shad has arrived. Maynard takes a travel mug from the counter and pours some hot coffee for himself. Then he grabs a few dog biscuits that he puts in the pocket of his navy-coloured wind breaker. "Where's her leash? And don't worry, we'll take good care of the little girl. Will even let her run off-leash if we're able."

Sandy retrieves Misty's leash from the closet and hands it to Maynard with a big smile. She scratches the dog's head and says, "You be a good girl, okay?"

The house feels a little less like home with Misty now out the door. "Holy. She's only been gone a minute and already it's so quiet in here," Sandy remarks.

"Oh, she's in good hands, Sandy. And it's probably good to socialize her with others, like when I walk her sometimes. Come," Charlene gestures towards the patio doors, "let's take our coffee outside. And bring the drums. I wanna see if I remember some of the songs from last night."

Sandy heads to the living room to retrieve the drums. Nina allowed the women to bring them home after the ceremony last evening. Charlene carries both their coffees outdoors. She notices her cousin's rhubarb growing near the back wooden fence and makes a mental note to pick it later today. It's likely to turn into a sweet crumble dessert served with cream for tonight's dinner. The rhubarb stalks are perfect for picking, narrow and not yet gone to seed. The plant is next to a bed of colourful dahlias that grow well in Saskatchewan's arid climate. Charlene smiles realizing that the way the petals are arranged looks like a small child has glued pasta shells together and then painted the flower a bright colour. Majestic poppies are also in full bloom near the back gate that leads to the alley. Their petals are so thin they are almost transparent. Charlene appreciates all the flowers and plants in Sandy's garden. The northern landscape is so different. Her few moments of quiet gratitude are interrupted by song. Sandy is sounding the vocals they'd learned the night before.

"How did that one go again?" Sandy hopes Charlene remembers the melody. "*Weh, weh, hey, weh oh/ Weh, weh, hey, weh hey weh oh*. Does that sound right?" Still inspired by the ceremony, she's trying to remember the sweet melody for the drum song called Grandmother Moon.

"Ah. That sounds great!" Char cries out.

And the two join in chorus: "*In the night sky we honour you Grandmother Moon. For you are the spirit of woman. Weya hey weh ho.*"

Nina had told them the song came from her Auntie who is an Elder in Manitoba. Nina's Auntie Jean had a vision about the song and the drum. In Auntie Jean's vision, a group of Grandmothers were singing the song on a hilltop. It was at dusk, just as the sun was setting. A windless evening with no clouds and no sounds other than the Grandmothers' song. Auntie Jean was instructed to teach the song to other women and to guide them to pick up the drum. She was told that eventually there needed to be as many women as there are leaves on trees singing and drumming—to return to balance.

"*Weya hey ah weh hey yo. I will not be afraid to say what I know anymore. For you, Grandmother Moon, I know are with me. Hey yo!*"

Their joyous song leaves Sandy and Charlene unaware that the front door bell is ringing, and there is no Misty around, who would normally alert Sandy that someone wants to visit.

So the guests at the doorway follow the small walk at the side of the house and let themselves in through a gated wooden fence which leads to the backyard.

Nina and Mary Ann startle the women who are lost in song in Sandy's backyard. "Sounding beautiful, ladies." Nina offers the compliment but her sudden appearance causes a shriek.

Charlene is startled and instinctively grabs the nearest item to throw. Same reaction she'd give to seeing a fox following too closely in the bush. Her aim is off and the crab apple which flies from her fist lands with a soft thud at Nina's sandal. The next joyous sound to be heard is hard laughter from the belly. Mary Ann is cackling so much that she loses her breath and begins to cough, "Water!" She's still wearing her ribbon skirt from the Moon Ceremony prompting Sandy and Charlene to realize that they didn't return their skirts after last night's ceremony nor did they offer to give them back. So they make that suggestion now.

Nina refuses. "They were a gift. Chances are good that now that you have begun learning, you will need them because there will be many more ceremonies where someone expects you to wear a skirt."

It makes Sandy think about some of the many friends and colleagues she has who never wear skirts. This brings to mind a question she longs to ask. Sandy briefly excuses herself to go inside and retrieve a package of tobacco from a drawer in her kitchen. She returns to the deck and turning toward the Elder, asks, "Nina, I have been wanting to ask you this for a long time. If a woman doesn't feel comfortable wearing a skirt, for whatever reason, does that exclude her from prayer and ceremony?"

"Oh, my girl, I am glad you asked because I have heard this concern many times." Nina states that Creator is satisfied that prayer is being offered at all, whether certain articles of clothing are worn or not. "Creator knows what is in the heart." This explanation gives Sandy clarity and a resolve to not push her beliefs onto someone if they are not ready or not able to do things the same way she does. Sandy does wear skirts and is thrilled to be able to keep the one made for her by Nina.

"There's some fresh coffee and some bannock left over from last night. If I warm it in the microwave a bit, it'll be softened again. I got some Saskatoon berry jam the other day too. Anyone want some?" Sandy offers.

Such an innocent question, but met with tears by Mary Ann. "I'm sorry. I seem to break down at any offer of kindness these days," Mary Ann confides. "It's just that I hardly recognize myself anymore. And everything reminds me of John. We used to go berry picking."

Charlene has already gone into the house and returns with a box of tissue. "It's all right to let the tears flow, Mary Ann. They do cleanse and allow you to let out whatever it is that you are carrying around and need to get rid of."

Mary Ann confides that she was first attracted to John because he seemed so rooted in spirituality. "That part of my life had always been empty, until I met John. He seemed to live in a good way. He knew the stories and talked of teachings and protocols. He took me to ceremony. It's why I fell in love with him. I trusted him, but I guess I moved too soon. I just wanted to find a place to belong, and I thought he was the person who would provide me that place."

Nina speaks up. "There are those who talk. And there are those who do not. The gifted ones never brag about what Creator has gifted to them. They are light workers, trying to turn the tide and heal the wounds without acknowledgement, without fanfare. There is no need to call attention to gifts given. There is only the need to develop the gift and pass it on to others. It is the practise of humility. Always be wary of someone who brags and constantly seeks attention and praise. They will usually leave you feeling empty by saying things like, 'I am holier than you. I am more worthy than you.' They might make you feel small. And that is simply wrong. I am sorry, Mary Ann, that you had to learn this harsh lesson. But now you know."

The women allow Mary Ann to vent as much as she needs to. She tells them she felt as though she was nothing more than another trophy. She knew it instinctively, but she never wanted to say out loud that John Wayne only wanted her so that he could show off his prowess with yet another younger woman. He liked that she did not drink and was not hooked on drugs. She sobs, describing how it fell apart so quickly. "I fell for him because he was always attentive and kind. We used to go for walks and we used to sit and chat for hours." But then, after a few short months of taking her places, and introducing her around, it all stopped. "He'd just plop himself on the couch at the end of the day and say he wanted to do 'all of nothing.' He stopped being physically intimate. Almost never touching me. We hardly ever had sex anymore. And when we did, it took all of one minute. He'd roll on and off just as quickly. Always made me wonder if he'd already turned to someone else? And, if I ever felt in the mood, he would make me feel like I was dirty to even suggest intimacy."

Mary Ann talks about how John Wayne spent his entire days out in the fishing shack, never including her in his life. She tells them he spent more time with friends at the pool hall and that his pushing her away was a form of emotional abuse. "I fell for his phony exterior," she sighs. "I feel like such a loser to have believed him. I should have known though. The signs were all there. He always demonized any partner who he'd been with in the past. Always blaming them. Even talking about the mother of his children like she was an evil entity. He told me he even purposely quit his job so that he wouldn't have to pay her child support. What kind of man does that? I suppose I should have known it was just a matter of time before he'd blame me, too, for things he did in the past, for everything."

"Normalized disfunction," Nina pipes up again. "So many of us have been treated so badly by so many people for such a long period of time, we accept abusive behaviour as though it's normal. Residential school priests and nuns made it their mission to treat us badly. Not all, but too many foster parents treated us like pets, or even like slaves. But the time has come for us to stop treating each other badly. We are out of the storm. We were told we were no good by way too many people who had no knowledge about anything we've gone through. And now that you recognize it for what it is, it's likely you won't ever accept it again."

Mary Ann as well as Sandy and Charlene nod in agreement.

"Good for you," Sandy says. "It is important to know that you are not the cause of his pain. That you have come to this realization has to do with courage. I hardly know him but I think that John Wayne lives a life shrouded in fear and he hides that behind the pretence that he has the gift of spiritual insight. I figured that out the moment I met him. What kind of person brags about going to a sweat lodge the first moment you meet him?"

"He's always been a talker. Talks mostly about himself." Charlene adds, "And I should know. I've known him my entire life."

There is a moment of silence and affirmation as the three women continue to comfort Mary Ann.

Nina touches Mary Ann's shoulder, offering more insight, "Our men, so many of them, are damaged. It's our women who rise above. Always have. We are the ones who raise the sons and daughters while these men run away, creating even more children and then abandoning them, too. Making children is the easy part. But never taking care of them once they are in the world, well, that's just wrong. Cowardly even. These kind of men run until they think they've found some answers, like John Wayne has. Which is good, but it comes too late, especially if they never own up to what they have done."

Nina pauses, then adds, "Fact is, we can no longer wait for the leaders. We are the leaders. We are the teachers. As women. We are the ones who our children can rely on. We are where they go to truly be safe. A fake healer? It happens too often. And it isn't real. So my prayer now is that you can somehow know. Maybe be wiser. Recognize that it is his fear, his pain, his cowardice that made him treat you badly. Not yours. But you will learn from this."

Nina remembers meeting Mary Ann for the first time and witnessing the deep bruising on her face and upper body. She tells Mary Ann that any man who equates violence with sex, may never be capable of expressing intimacy. "But, most importantly, you need to stop blaming yourself." They share a hug, more profound than any physical touch Mary Ann ever remembers sharing with John Wayne. Or any man for that matter.

Mary Ann wipes a tear and excuses herself from where everyone is congregated in the backyard. "I need to go to the washroom," she whispers. She makes her way indoors, through the back deck and into Sandy's kitchen. Being with these women has given her strength. Mary Ann finds herself saying another quiet prayer of gratitude as she walks down the hallway that leads to the stairwell. It is a moment of solace that ends abruptly. By chance, she glances outside, through the bevelled glass on the front door.

She gasps, then stops short, frozen with fear. John Wayne is parking his vehicle on the curb directly in front of Sandy's home.

47. MY HAND WILL NOT TOUCH YOU

MOMENTS OF PURE ENLIGHTENMENT can never be described in words. It's like floating on clouds, where the soul is dancing, opening a portal to experience joy in the present moment. Basking in the warmth of the morning sun as it climbs the sky, Sandy continues to relax on the back deck humming and holding a rattle in her hand. It too is precious, thinks Sandy, remembering Charlene's story about that rattle.

"I don't even know where that rattle came from," Char said during one of their long walks with Misty. "And I always wondered why Nikawiy never fixed that rattle. But when I heard the story, I understood why she didn't."

Sandy gazes at the outline of a heart. It is the pattern in which the deer rawhide settled after being gnawed on by Char as a baby. Charlene says it was a gift given to their mother when Charlene was born. No store bought item but crafted by hand out of willow and sinew. Inside, small pebbles from the Puskwakau River were placed to create sound. The head of the rattle was thick and round upon crafting but it didn't stay that way for long. Baby Charlene started chewing on it when she started to teethe. It collapsed the rawhide that had long ago dried into this heart-shaped image. "Mom always said she could have soaked the rawhide again to puff it up and make it round, but she never did. Said that heart shape held a cherished memory. A tie between mother and daughter and life. It's a good story."

They are interrupted by brash sound. "Hey! What's going on? The morning coven?" John Wayne has made his way in to the backyard through the side gate, unnoticed. "I rang the doorbell but I guess you didn't hear it, so I let myself in, cousin." He turns towards Charlene, and holds up a large paper bag. "Brought some wihkaskwapoy to remind you of home."

"Oh," a startled Charlene replies, "John. What a surprise. We weren't expecting you. Why didn't you call?"

"No need for that. Family doesn't need to ask." John glances around the backyard, and grimaces upon seeing Nina holding a drum. "Besides, I know I'm one of your favourite people. Always happy to see me. Everyone is happy to see me. It's how I roll. And, I have to admit as much as I like seeing you, I came to take Maynard for lunch. I wanted to surprise everyone. Where is Maynard?"

John Wayne gives no one a chance to answer before taking a seat beside Sandy. "I'm in the city for an education conference." He tells them the Chiefs are meeting with provincial education officials and he's there to advocate for the On The Land programs.

"That's admirable," Nina says, offering him a cup of coffee.

John was invited to discuss a plan to introduce teachings of the land to the provincial curriculum. It's something he's been doing up north, taking groups of young students to the bush. Teaching them how to build a fire and a quinzee (in winter) or a survival shelter made with sticks during other seasons. He also shows them how to snare and gut a rabbit, and how to fish by fashioning willow branches and soaking bark to make string. Things he himself learned from Uncle Gabriel. "I even teach them how to make campfire bannock because they'll need it if they ever get around to cooking a fish."

Charlene chuckles. It is common knowledge where she's from to never eat fish without first having a slice of bannock nearby. That way if someone missed a bone when cleaning that fish, that bone won't get caught in the throat because the bannock is heavy enough to push it down.

"Those kids need to learn these things just as much as math and reading. I teach all age groups..." John Wayne stops short, motioning to the drum which Nina still holds, "But one thing I would never bring to the students is a drum like that. There are girls present. And a girl, or a woman, is never allowed to hold a drum. Not even touch it."

Charlene gasps audibly. Her hand twitches uncomfortably and she spills a bit of her coffee on her skirt. It's followed by stunned silence. Sandy shakes her head and drops her gaze to the ground rather than meeting John Wayne's accusing eyes. Nina, in her wisdom, does not react negatively nor does she object to his comment. Rather, she slowly raises her drum high and she begins to play. The drum beats are slow and methodical. Eerily enchanting, as though they are calling the spirits. Nina sings a prayer song. The same song she has been teaching the others at the shelter. A song that she sang to Grandmother Moon last night. Sandy and Charlene join in chorus.

It is not an act of defiance. It is an act of resilience and inclusion.

When the song ends, it is John Wayne's turn to gasp. He runs his fingers over his long braid and closes his eyes and whispers loud enough for everyone to hear, "Dancing with the devil."

Charlene jumps up. "That's uncalled for," she chastises. "I haven't said anything to you before, but what you just said is so disrespectful and uncalled for."

A quick sound escapes from Nina, who seems like she might add to this discussion, but Charlene is feeling stronger since being away from her routine up north, and away from John Wayne's way of thinking. She adds, "You're always talking about yourself as though you are the only one who understands traditions and teachings. Belittling anyone who has a different opinion from yours."

Sandy watches the exchange between them and is stunned. She has never seen her sister so angry, and she knows she cannot interrupt.

Surprised by her words and not sure how to react, because Charlene's never challenged him before, John leans forward and states, "All I ever do is work for the people. To strengthen our culture."

"Yes, you ass. And so you think." Her cheeks are flushed with anger.

John sinks back into his chair as Charlene continues, "You tell people what you think they want to hear. But I don't want to hear another bit of horse shit from you about anything! Just because you quit drinking doesn't make you an authority on goodness, or on anything else, for that matter."

John Wayne clenches his fist and for a moment Charlene wonders if he's posing to strike her. He's done it before.

Charlene rails, "That's right. Get mad. It's what you do. Bet you never show that side to all those people you preach at. And the children you've abandoned. Ever tell your followers that you named your boys Cash and Kerry because you thought it was funny? They were bullied all the time. Not that you'd know. You left that family with nothing. Auntie Myrna and I had to bring food to them once they finally found a place in Prince Albert. They were starving and you didn't do a thing to help. But, I am pretty sure in your ceremonies you talk about the sacredness of family and what a great father you are. Tugeye!"

It is Nina's turn to gasp, at hearing Charlene utter a Cree swear word, inappropriate in any conversation. John Wayne or not. "Sister," she says calmly and she places her hand on Charlene's shoulder. "It's good to get things off your chest. But the whole teaching of respect starts with yourself."

"I'm sorry, Nina, it just came out."

But her eyes are fixed on John Wayne. "You showed up here unannounced and uninvited. And, I know it's usual for us to extend a welcome because you are family. But, you're not welcome here, John. You need to go." She pauses, takes a breath, then adds firmly, "And I mean go now!"

Everyone is in agreement with the suggestion, including John Wayne himself. But before he leaves, Nina thinks it important to add something else to the discussion. "And as for you," Nina says and turns her attention to John, "you need to stop pretending because you are causing harm to others and it'll come back on you."

But John Wayne is one of those people who always has to have the last word, even if it's a stupid one, "No. You're the one playing with fire," he says to Nina, "and it'll come back on you, you witch."

Nina is unshaken. "I've never met someone who calls himself a healer and then refers to an Elder as a witch. But, I must say, I am proudly practiced in the art of bitch-craft."

"What?" John didn't expect such a response.

"You heard me," Nina says coldly. "I am guilty of bitch-craft, which viewed another way means telling it like it is. Even if you don't want to hear it. And, yes, apparently your cousin is well-versed, too."

It is Charlene's cue. "You heard her. Piss off already and take your ego with you! That's right," Char is on a roll, "it seems to me that one of the worst curses a person can carry is to worry about what everyone thinks about you and what you do. Talk about shit coming back on you. Cha!"

Charlene longs to say something about the harm he has caused Mary Ann but her instinct advises her to remain silent. He doesn't know she is here. Instead, Charlene waves her arms towards John Wayne, a signal that leaves no room for doubt. It is time for him to leave.

John scoffs, turns and strides out the same side gate from where he appeared.

Once he is gone, and the women hear his truck tires screech away, Nina suggests, "Not sure what just happened, but, we'll have to smudge." While she retrieves a few items from the small pouch she's carrying, a timid Mary Ann slowly makes her way back out to the deck where the women still stand in disbelief.

"He gone?" she asks.

She's been hiding in the upstairs bathroom this entire time.

48. RAISED ON ROBBERY

JOHN WAYNE IS NOT FAMILIAR with the City of Regina. He curses the large flow of traffic on busy Albert Street as he turns north off the 13th Avenue market area where Sandy lives. His fist throbs, having hammered it on the dashboard a few times since being put in his place moments ago. "Bitches," he continues cursing to himself, "and that old bitch is the worst. Teaching those women to question my authority." He sneers, both because of his dark thoughts and because another driver has just cut him off. John flips him the bird then chortles, "She's probably an old lesbian to boot. Bitches. They'll get theirs, just wait and see," he promises to no one.

He's in a bit of a quandry though, having gone to Sandy's house and hoping to find a place to bunk down for the next couple of days. "A visit with that fairy cousin of mine would have been nice. At least Maynard isn't involved in this bullshit." John Wayne didn't bring a lot of cash with him, so staying at an expensive hotel, where the Chiefs might be, is out of the question.

John Wayne's thoughts turn to Mary Ann. He didn't get the chance to ask Charlene or Sandy if they'd seen her lately. "She's a fucking bitch, too. Just taking off like that." His anger oozes from his pores and he wipes away the perspiration from his brow. He had spent the past couple of days going from bar to bar to coffee shop in Prince Albert and in Saskatoon. Stalking places Mary Ann used to talk about. Sleeping in his pick up at night. But she wasn't in any of those places. That's when it occurred to him that she might have fled to Regina and then he thought about Sandy. A familiar face. A face he now hates.

It's while he's driving near the intersection at Albert Street and South Railway that John makes up his mind to stop and sit for a bit. And so a decision is made: he'll stay at the Empire Hotel. A place notorious for drugs and hookers and trouble, but it is cheap to rent a room. Cheap and most likely to be memorable.

The parking spaces beside this hotel are small but John manages to wedge his truck in between a rusted beige-coloured K-Car and a dented green AMC Gremlin. "Fuck!" He cusses again, realizing there is hardly any room for him to inch his body out from the cab of the truck. His door is only able to open about ten inches before striking the rubbing strip of the K-Car. He doesn't care if that unsightly vehicle gets another dent or scrape from him. Once his foot hits pavement, John Wayne's sense of smell is assaulted by many variables: feces, urine, the greasy smell of fried food, and exhaust fumes. The sounds he's used to hearing back home, like the wind in the pines, are replaced by the honking of horns and unending rush of traffic. That is, until he hears a voice call. "Hey bro! Spare some change? I need to buy some food. I'm hungry."

It is a homeless man, clearly drunk and wearing soiled trousers, holding out his hand. He smells bad even from ten feet away. John acknowledges the man with a wave but decides he doesn't want to give him any money. Instead, and with some effort, John Wayne reaches into his truck cab and grabs a leftover sandwich that he'd packed earlier in the day and hadn't gotten around to eating. "It's spam and mustard," John tells him. "It'll stick to your ribs."

As he tries to hand the sandwich over, the street person slaps it out of his hands, "I am not a beggar, you asshole."

"But you told me you are hungry." John is clearly confused.

People saying what they think you want to hear.

John Wayne makes his way to the lobby. The pronounced smell of cigarette smoke provides the initial greeting upon entering the dimly lit space. The orange-coloured couch in the lobby looks as though some springs are damaged. It sags towards the middle and the cushions are visibly dirty and worn. John spots a sign that reads: *Rooms by the night or by the hour – rates vary.*

There is no one at the front desk, so John rings the small bell in front of him. Glancing around the lobby, he notices ashtrays that no one has taken the time to empty. A small black-and-white television set is broadcasting an afternoon soap opera from a shadowy corner that leads to a staircase. John's train of thought is suddenly interrupted by someone's thick Newfoundland accent, "Help yuh, by?"

"Ah? Yes." John Wayne rents a room for two nights.

"I'm gonna need an extra two dollars for the use of these," the clerk indicates, as he passes him two shabby towels. "There's a shared bathroom on either end of the hallway upstairs, but there is also a sink in each room in case you wanna put in a shave in the morning."

Once in the room, John thinks about unpacking his small travel bag. It's always in his truck and carries the essentials: a hunting knife, basic survival gear, clean socks, and a notepad and pen. He's left the ribbon shirt he's planning to wear for the education meeting wrapped in a paper bag and under the passenger seat of his truck. Figures it's likely safer there. The only lock for the door is a dull butter knife that gets jammed into a space between the door itself and the flimsy molding. The butter knife sits atop an equally flimsy plywood desk near the bed. It gives John pause, and he elects to hide his travel bag under the metal bed frame.

He checks himself in the mirror that hangs crookedly above the small sink. And then he pokes at his ear and picks out wax. Then he sniffs the ear wax before heading back downstairs to the bar. He remembers someone once telling him that when a person produces excessive ear wax it may be an indication of some type of imbalance. Naturally, John Wayne doesn't believe this would apply to him.

He doesn't drink anymore. It's true. But that doesn't necessarily mean he's also given up other bad behaviours, which were partnered with the alcohol. Bad habits have always led him to bad situations.

49. CONDIE REFUGE

MAYNARD IS DELIGHTED TO BE GREETED by a flock of pelicans wading through the shallow waters that dot the landscape of Condie Refuge. They generally prefer nesting in large bodies of water, so it's a surprise to find them here. Condie Nature Refuge is a conservation area close to the City of Regina, and where Shad has brought Maynard and Misty for the afternoon.

Father, are you here? Maynard asks himself, remembering a conversation he had with Gabriel last summer.

See those pelicans, my son? Old Gabriel asks of Maynard. My old Mooshum told me that when a pelican crosses your path, it is a sign that you need to take some time for yourself. Go inward to see what it really is you need to find balance. Allow forgiveness to flow through you.

"Penny for your thoughts, my friend." Shad brings Maynard back to the present moment.

"Oh, just thinking about my dad is all," Maynard says, and attaches the pink leash to Misty's collar, "I just miss him. We spent so much time out on the land. Being here reminds me of him." Maynard pauses for a moment to regain his composure, "And, thanks for getting me away from the city. It's good to visit, but wouldn't want to live there."

"I know what you mean," Shad says. "I do like the city. But I feel more at home when we go to the cottage up north. And thank God we go there. Otherwise, I wouldn't have met you."

"What are the chances that you'd be selling us sandwiches that snowy afternoon and then we'd see each other at that cowboy bar? And now, both be walking here together, all these months later?"

"There is no chance, Maynard," Shad replies. "I think we were destined to meet."

A tender moment. They look at each other and both smile tentatively.

"Bring your camera?" Shad asks, breaking the spell.

"I did," Maynard replies. "But, just this disposal one. Never used one like this before. Hope it takes good pictures." From his jacket pocket Maynard retrieves the small camera. "You and Misty can be the first on this film reel. Take her leash and go stand over there," Maynard suggests and points towards a bluff that is already a perfect frame for the photograph. Vast pink sky, flocks of song birds perched in willows add harmony. Shad poses by spreading both arms wide, welcoming the moment.

"Now, what about you?"

"Whaddaya mean?" Maynard asks.

"Fancy a picture with you and Misty?" By this time, Shad has let the dog off her leash. It is a perfect day for walking. Because the trails are quiet, there is a measure of privacy. Misty has run to a small pond in the distance. "We have to catch her first," Maynard laughs. "But these days, I'm not much for pictures." He runs his fingers through his hair. "It's still in that in-between stage so my hair just looks a mess. Holy. How long does it take to grow a braid anyway? Feels like I've been trying to grow it forever."

"I disagree," Shad laughs. "Bet I could fashion it into a braid. It seems long enough."

The sit together quietly on the bluff. Gingerly, Shad separates Maynard's locks into three strands and begins to braid. He has watched his little sister do it many times and he attempts to copy her. It is going well. In the meantime, Maynard is dumbfounded. Shad's fingers feel so much like the wind moving through his hair. "Voilà!" Shad smiles then reaches into Maynard's jacket pocket to grab the disposable camera. He snaps a photo, "You know how I think you look? Brave and proud and handsome."

It is another tender moment.

This time Misty interrupts them by running back to them and then jumping happily at Maynard. Jump, jump, jump. She wants him to play with her. Shad finds an elastic band in his jacket pocket so that the braid he's just fashioned doesn't come loose.

"Why do you carry an elastic?" Maynard inquires.

Shad clears his throat. "I don't always. It's just that I haven't worn this coat since the last time we were up north at the cabin. When we came home, first thing I did was go and get the mail. A little bundle of letters, mostly bills, were wrapped by this elastic."

Maynard runs his hand over the tight braid as the two resume their walk towards a scenic gully, the ground covered with colourful wild flowers. Maynard tells Shad he's been determined to grow his hair since his father passed. "Didn't realize it was long enough. Thank you, Shad. Ever since I moved back in with my dad, after my mom died, my cousin has been helping me learn about our own culture."

"What do you mean, learning about your own culture?" Shad interjects.

Maynard gives Shad a short history lesson on how the residential school system disrupted spiritual beliefs and family traditions and ties. "Everyone had short hair at residential school and they were taught that our beliefs were bad, including wearing a braid." Maynard continues, explaining that his cousin, John Wayne, has tried reintroducing spiritual practices to many of the people back home. "He's the one who suggested I grow my hair. He says there is power in uncut hair. He says a braid represents unity and connection to the tall grasses of

Mother Earth. So he encouraged me to grow my hair, but Dad didn't like it. Said it made me look like a girl. I almost got it cut again," Maynard says. "But now that he's in heaven with Mom, maybe wearing a braid will somehow keep me connected to both of my parents." When Maynard pauses, Shad notices that Misty seems to have found something at water's edge.

They both walk over to the pond and Maynard spots something familiar. Something, taught to him by John Wayne. It's a kind of grass, unique-looking and sturdy, taller than the other indigenous plants. There is some purple colouring near the shaft of the grass blades. "Misty has found us some sweetgrass," he says and smiles broadly.

50. FROM THE SHADOWS CAME

"WELL, WELL, PRETTY MISTER. Look at you, all shiny and clean. Please tell me you are not here with your wife." Hell of a way to introduce yourself, but it's exactly the way Miss Purdy introduces herself.

John Wayne is not expecting such an attractive young woman to notice him as he sits alone in this dingy bar that reeks of spilled beer and cigarettes, and the accompanying lies and sin. "Pardon me?" Is all he can think to say, having been taken aback by her brash opening.

"My name is Purdy." She holds out her hand as if she wants him to kiss it. "Mind if I sit with you?"

"Please do." John Wayne hurriedly pulls an empty chair closer to where he's seated and motions for her to join him. He's proud that he somehow managed to attract her attention and he sits up higher in his chair. Because he is narcissistic enough to believe that his company is a gift to women, he doesn't realize Purdy is there for reasons of business only. "This sounds like a cliché," John begins, "but do you come here often?"

"Often enough," she responds, draping herself artfully on the small, wobbly chair so that John can see where her black fishnet stockings end and the fun might begin. Her complexion is the colour of alabaster. Her lipstick, bright red. "Buy me a drink?" she asks and pulls a cigarette from inside her bra.

"Here, let me get that for you," John offers. "I don't smoke but I do spend a lot of time out on the land. Gotta have one of these to light a fire." He flicks his black Bic lighter, and asks, "And what would you like to drink?"

But there is no need for a response, nor for anyone to take an order. Before John Wayne has finished lighting the woman's cigarette, the tired waitress has already placed Purdy's drink in front of her. "Bit early, even for you Purdy. Here's your vodka and ice. A double of course. The gentleman paying, is he?" She is chewing gum with her mouth open. A plastic nametag on her beige uniform indicates her name is Marsha. She has a pronounced British accent and appears to be in her early thirties. No ring on her finger. It makes John wonder what circumstances might have caused her to work in this dark place? Maybe she's in Canada illegally? The thought crosses his mind.

"Oh, yes, of course." John Wayne agrees, "Can I put it on a tab?"

"We don't run tabs here," Marsha explains, "but I can take a twenty from you now and keep a run from there. Sound good?"

John nods and hands her a twenty-dollar bill. "Do you have any food here?"

"None that I'd recommend," the waitress giggles. "But I can bring you a menu. Pretty safe if you stick to the basics, like fries or soup. Comes from a can. Can't go wrong with that." Any good waitress, even in a place like this, knows her customers. It's why Marsha glances at Purdy's glass before leaving the table. "So? No nursin' today I see. Fancy another double, Purd's? I can fetch one on the way back when I bring the menu." She turns her attention to John Wayne. "And you, sir, another 7 Up?" He nods in agreement.

Two doubles, too early in the day can add up to to a lot of trouble, thinks John, unless Miss Purdy slows down. She doesn't. Marsha brings her a second drink within minutes and Purdy shoots it back. "Let's dance," she says, while pulling back her red chiffon blouse that is unbuttoned far enough to reveal a lacy pale pink bra. "And, I'll have another one, Marsha. Make sure it's here by the time we finish our dance."

There is no real dance floor. Just a spot of roughed-up hard-wood near the jukebox. "Gimme a quarter, cowboy. I'll find something nice and romantic."

John hands the young woman a coin and watches her as she slides her torso across the top of the juke box, squinting at the song titles below the rounded and scratched plexiglass. She wears four-inch heels to make her appear taller, on a frame that would otherwise be described as petite. With her hair pulled back in a tight ponytail, John can't help but think that Purdy looks no older than the students he takes out on the land, back home. "Come on. What's your name again?" Purdy stumbles into John Wayne's arms.

"Oh, John's my name. Thought I already told you."

"John, eh? You shittin' me or is that your real name?" She doesn't look him in the eye asking the query. Indeed, the two haven't made eye contact since Purdy invited herself to sit at John's table.

"No, I am not making it up. That's my real name."

"Fitting," she responds.

Even though the song Purdy chose is a fast one, Purdy insists on dancing slow, "Keep your strong arms around me, John. You feel so warm." She lays her head on his chest, "You wanna stay here in the bar and eat french fries? Or you wanna go somewhere more private to eat pussy? We can have our own private party and dance in any position you desire." Purdy breathes the words into John's left ear.

He is not familiar with a young woman being so forcefully suggestive, but John decides he likes her assertiveness. He pulls her closer so she can feel his erection.

"But wait. Before we go up, I assume you have a room here but if you don't, you should get one," she slurs.

"I have a room." John assures her, holding her hand and leading her to the door.

"But, no," Purdy hesitates, "before we go up, I need to know if you have the money."

"The money?" John is perplexed but then he figures she is talking about ordering some food and coming back down to the bar later. "Oh, yeah. I've got money, don't worry about that."

"Okay then. Let's do this." Before leaving the bar, Purdy returns to the table to chug her latest double. She grabs John Wayne by his long braid and leds him through the upstairs corridor. "Which room number, John?"

"It's this one here," he says and opens the door.

She stumbles over the threshold, swearing, "Goddamn. Just about broke a heel." John Wayne ignores her remark and cups her small oval-shaped face in both hands, as if to kiss her. She stops him, "Awww. I should have ordered another drink to bring up here. Don't suppose you have a stash, do ya'?"

John doesn't drink but he remembers the bottle of double distilled 100-proof moonshine that's in his travel bag. It's something he always carries in the case of a hunting accident out on the land, in case a wound needs dressing. It'll work just fine in this situation too. This is, after all, an accident waiting to happen.

Purdy watches, waiting for a taste, as John pours the murky liquid into a clear plastic glass which sits by the small sink in his room. The moonshine doesn't smell rank. It doesn't really smell at all, but John knows it will do the trick.

She's already tipsy, he thinks to himself, one shot of this and she'll be out. *And then I can help myself. No memories from her. No objections to playtime. No witnesses to say otherwise. Like it never happened.*

He hands her a full glass. It would amount to four shots or even more if they were still back at the bar, "Here you go, my beauty. I think you'll enjoy this. Special home-tested recipe."

Purdy accepts the plastic cup, inspects the liquid, then sniffs at it. "Smells like potato water. The kind my granny uses to make gravy."

John manages a sinister smile and says, "Go ahead. It'll warm you from the inside."

Purdy shoots back the 100-proof not realizing the ramifications. This is no store bought vodka. "Here, let me take off those pretty shoes of yours," John Wayne offers. "I can even rub your feet, if they feel tired."

It takes only moments for the moonshine to produce what John hoped as a desired effect. Purdy's limp body, now passed out in his bed and vulnerable, slumps across a tattered old bedspread. He moves her towards the middle of the bed, so he can see her legs spread and he removes her stockings.

He pushes his index finger inside her warmth to feel a slippery wetness. John Wayne's pulse rate increases as does his breathing. As he gets more excited, he puts two more fingers up her muff. That's when he notices a tattoo, just above the pubic bone and where her tuft of hair begins: *LA Pussy.*

John Wayne knows that First Nations people from the La Ronge area of Northern Saskatchewan often refer to where they live as LA. He wonders if this is Purdy's stomping grounds too.

It turns him on even further knowing someone stuck pins so near to her private parts. It would have hurt and he enjoys pleasure and pain side by side. He wants to inflict pain, too; he wants to see her throbbing, sore nipples rise full and red, as though they'd been rubbed by sand paper. But John remembers, he didn't carry the usual clothes pins in his travel bag. He checks the side drawer in the makeshift desk beside the bed.

In the drawer is a bible, which someone has read because inside the pages of the bible, he finds some large paperclips that have been used to mark passages. Psalm 139: *But even in darkness I cannot hide from you.* John Wayne grabs the paperclips, feeling the grip of the cold metal. He carefully pulls Purdy's blouse from her body, being careful not to damage the light chiffon material. He undoes her bra, which has a clasp at the front. He pinches her nipples and grunts, sounding like he's lifting something heavy. When her nipples are hard, John fastens the paper clips to each nipple. Immediately, the surrounding areola begins to turn red. He can see throbbing as the clips begin to move with each beat of her heart.

It's time for him to move as well. John Wayne unfastens the belt he's wearing. He fashions it into a noose and then slips it over Purdy's head and neck and attaches to the old metal bed post. Again, he grunts. This time louder. "You fucking bitch. You little slut. Cunt, you cunt, now you are mine!" He hisses this diatribe into the ear of his unconscious victim and forces his hardened weapon into her with such force that the young girl twitches even though she is unconscious. John Wayne continues: "Little white pussy. I'll fuck you, bitch. I'll fuck you so hard that you can't walk tomorrow." He fixates on her pulsating nipple and moves faster and harder, continuing to grunt, louder now, then starting to growl.

He is oblivious to the sound of someone banging at the door.

But by the time John Wayne realizes he neglected to put the butter knife in the space between the door and the moulding, it's too late.

51. NO SECRET PLACES

"I CAN'T BELIEVE I WAS SO NAIVE. I just wanted to find somewhere to belong and John seemed ... well, seemed like he had it together. How could I be so stupid?" Mary Ann is still visibly shaken by his surprise visit. She sobs, feeling shameful that she allowed him to go over the line with her too, in ways that he wrapped up in a bow. Her memory goes to her pubic hair.

It's growing back, but not without inevitable complications. Pimple-like welts have appeared that are painful for her to squeeze in order for the hair to find its way out. *Let me tweeze the area into the shape of a heart. It'll prove how much you love me.* She remembers him saying just before he plucked the area with a cold tweezer. It hurt and made Mary Ann flinch. There was even a bit of bleeding and John seemed to enjoy the anguish he inflicted.

"Even when I started crying and begged him to stop, he wouldn't. Said if I loved him, I would allow him to pluck my pubes in the shape of a heart."

She says he spent too much time treating her like an object to be played with and much less time treating her as a woman. She remembers a day when the water truck arrived late. There was not much left in the tank, and she needed a shower, "I can't even wash my hair," Mary Ann had remarked, to which John had replied, "Don't need it. There's enough for a PTA to take care of what's really important."

Mary Ann needed clarification, "What does that mean?"

"It means we have enough water to wash your pussy, tits, and ass. Like I said, the parts that are important." Then he grabbed her by the ass and made grunting sounds like a pig. It was meant as a joke, but even still, Mary Ann can't understand why any respectful man would ever think a comment like that was funny.

"Don't beat yourself up, Mary Ann," Charlene consoles. "A lot of people think him to be real. They believe him when he talks so earnestly about medicine wheel teachings, which only encourage goodness. And they are impressed when he tells them that he runs a sweat lodge. But, I know better. Known him all my life. It's the reason I lost it."

She turns to Nina. "And I am sorry I swore. I've just been silent for so long. But when he basically attacked you, for being you and for helping us, well, that was just too much."

"No need to apologize, child." Nina hugs Charlene. "But what we need to do now, is eat. Sandy pre-heat your oven. I'm gonna make some bannock." She pauses, then asks, "Do you have an apron?"

Sandy has never owned one but makes a mental note to pick one up for what she hopes will become regular visits. Nina makes do with a large dishtowel that she tucks into the waistband of her skirt.

Like the woman herself, Nina's recipe for bannock is unique. She adds milk instead of water, which gives the bannock a bit of lift and makes it more fluffy. And, she uses yeast instead of baking soda, making her bannock more the consistency of a hearty loaf of bread. She also adds a hint of sugar to sweeten it.

While she is mixing all the dry ingredients together, Nina suddenly feels faint. Something—or someone—has arrived to show her something. Maybe it's Bushman?

Nina is forced to hold onto the kitchen counter with flour-covered hands. Before falling, she closes her eyes, lifting her head towards some unseen portal. She begins to sweat as images come in to her mind. She mouths the words as shadows appear in this vision. Some of those words come out as a whisper:

Young girl. Roberta. Didn't ask for trouble. John Wayne there. Darkness surrounds. The girl is crying but not aware. Clothespin. But there is some light. It comes from outside. Bushman watching through the window. Shape-shifter. He wears antlers.

Nina collapses on the kitchen floor.

"Oh my God! Nina. Nina!" A worried Sandy is the first to hear the glass bowl smashing to the floor. Flour everywhere. "Quick! Charlene, there is an ice pack in the freezer. We need to put it on her forehead."

As Char retrieves the cold pack, Mary Ann sobs even harder, "It's my fault, isn't it? I brought bad energy to your home and somehow summoned that bad man along with it."

"Don't talk like that," Sandy says. "Don't even think like that." She turns her attention back to Nina, who opened her eyes as soon as she discerned the coldness of the ice pack on her brow.

"I'm okay, my girl. Just went somewhere for a moment. It happens sometimes. No need to worry."

"Should we call an ambulance?" Charlene is already standing by the telephone.

"No need," Nina smiles reassuringly. "Like I said, this happens once in a while. But, usually, not so quickly. Guess I should have smudged harder." She lets out a little giggle and turns her attention to Mary Ann. "They told me you need a name. It will help protect you, Mary Ann."

Mary Ann gasps. She knows what Nina is saying, having been told by John Wayne the significance of a spirit name. "But, I'm not worthy, Nina."

"All the more reason," Nina says, now sitting on the floor. "Help me up," she says to Sandy. "I've ruined the bannock."

Then with the voice of wisdom she declares, "It's time to start over. For all of us."

No one is quick to react. Instead, they let the moment settle. Until the phone rings.

52. ANGEL AND THE BADMAN

"SO? WHAT DO WE HAVE HERE?" A query accompanied with a smirk. Two young thugs swing open the door to John Wayne's room, unannounced and unwelcomed.

"Some old man playing hide the salami with someone young enough to be his daughter, that's what."

"Who the hell are you? Get out now!" John Wayne shouts. He never expected the two hooligans to barge into his rented and unholy hideaway. His hard on deflates as quickly as his ire rises. "You have the wrong room. And, I'm kind of busy. So get out!"

The men do not move. Their faces are not covered although each of them wears a red bandana covering their hair. John quickly surmises they are Native. They speak with an accent and seem to be in their late twenties. Both have square jaws and several visible tattoos.

"No, old man. That's our girl you're bangin'," the taller hoodlum points to an incoherent Purdy, still chained to the bedpost. He slowly removes a handgun from inside the denim jacket he wears. "Get off her now or you'll get a taste of this, old man, ripped right up your ass." His voice is steady and authoritative. John shudders upon seeing the gun. He studies the weapon and thinks it might be a World War II service pistol. He wonders if it is stolen. As a hunter, he knows the finality of what this gun represents. He does as told, rolling away from young Purdy.

It isn't until this moment that John realizes that Purdy isn't just a young piece of tail who was flirting and trying to pick him up at the bar, as was his first thought. When he used to frequent places like this he used to score all the time. But going to bars was no longer part of his life. He only did it today to stop and think about what he was going to do next. Plot is more like it. He was ego-driven and wanted to put those women in their place. His own family! Until the young woman arrived and his small head took over.

His first response now is to grab for his trousers but he stops short when he feels the cold barrel touching his shoulder.

"No. Leave the pants. We want you to keep your pecker where we can see it."

Again John Wayne does as instructed, sitting naked from the waist down, at the end of the bed. The condom he's wearing falls off now that he is no longer erect.

The tall one seems to be the leader of these two, instructing his partner in crime to check on Purdy. "Hey, Levoy, look what he's done to her. Putting that belt around her neck. *Tsk, tsk.*" He slaps John Wayne so hard on the back of his head that it causes some spittle to fly from his mouth.

But before the one called Levoy goes to aid the girl, he stops short near the sink and mirror, where he sees the open flask. He sniffs it, grimacing at the smell and then takes a short swig. "Homemade. And good quality too, I can tell. But totally dangerous for our young Miss Purdy. Look what this moonshine did to her, you old perv!" Levoy grabs John Wayne by the braid, yanking his head towards the spot where Purdy continues to lie still on the bed. "And, what up with the paper clips, man? That shits gotta hurt. Like to see you try it."

"That's a great idea," the tall one nods in agreement, motioning that Levoy remove the paper clips from Purdy's nipples. "I say we put those clips on grandpa's foreskin here. Look!" He motions towards John Wayne's flaccid shaft. "The turtle has gone back into its shell. I say, we use those clips to make sure that turtle doesn't pop its head out again for a while."

"No, please. She's unharmed. And I have money. You can have it." John points towards his pants pocket. After unbuckling the belt around Purdy's neck, Levoy covers her with a sheet and moves to the other side of the bed to check John's pocket. He removes a wallet that is thick with bills. "Mostly twenties," he says, removing most of the money and jamming it in the front pocket of his jeans, "I will leave you some though," Levoy does not take the last bill in John's wallet, a fifty-dollar bill. "We might be criminals but at least we have some good qualities. You might need gas money. My guess is you ain't from around here."

John's head hangs; he is staring at the floor. But for a moment he glances up at Levoy and notices a strange tattoo on his neck. *LA Rules.* John knows that some from Northern Saskatchewan refer to the Town of La Ronge as LA. And he's heard stories that inmates sometimes adorn themselves with a tattoo like this. It makes him wonder if these two have ever spent time in the Prince Albert maximum security penitentiary? The girl on the bed has the same tattoo. Is this a coincidence? No coincidence.

"So ... Grandpa? What's this?" Levoy spies John Wayne's travel bag, still tucked under the bed. He unzips the tote, noticing the large hunting knife, "Jack pot!" Levoy removes the blade from its protective sheath, unnerving John with his next comment, "Whaddya say we try it out on Gramps here?"

"Go ahead. No skin off my ass," the tall one nods in agreement.

Levoy comes at John Wayne with the knife. But he doesn't cut him. Instead, he does something even more painful. With one swift flick, Levoy chops off John Wayne's long braid. "I know what this braid signifies to the world, you old asshole." He holds the braid up like a trophy, "Love, honour, and respect. But you are a fuckin' phony and don't deserve to wear this."

"Ha!" the tall one sniggers, "kinda like scalping the enemy," and he high fives Levoy, who is still holding John's braid. "It'll be put to good use. My cousin has cancer and just went through chemo. Something like this will make a nice wig."

Levoy may just as well have amputated John's right arm. That braid was his source of dignity. John's facial expression turns ashen and any fear that may have been visible in his eyes now turns to grief. An actual tear finds its way out. Neither bandit notices though because just then a raucous fart seeps from the body of the still-passed-out Purdy. Levoy holds his nose, "Damn girl! Not again." He protests as wet, runny, and smelly diarrhea oozes onto the sheet. The young naked prostitute has shit herself. "Not again. Second time this month. Damn alcoholics. We'll have to force her to eat more or turn her to pills so she stops shitting herself when she's passed out."

Levoy goes to the sink and grabs a washcloth. He soaks it in warm water and cleans her up. He throws the shit-stained cloth at John Wayne. It lands on his lap. Next, Levoy covers the nude girl with an extra blanket from the small closet, "Hey asshole. You can pay for the extra cleaning charges and the theft of a blanket. No one. And I mean no one fucks with us. Remember that because we will remember your face." Then he turns to his friend and adds, "I think we ought to leave this dude with something more to remember us by. And a notice to never fuck with one of our girls ever again."

The tall one spots a sewing kit, which is also in John's travel pack. He takes the kit out and begins to ready the needle with black thread. "Levoy, you hold this kitty," he says, handing the pistol over. "I notice you have sundance scars, old man. Can see them through your open shirt."

The tall one's memory travels back to his own boyhood, when his grandfather used to take him to ceremony. The sundance. A four-day, outdoor ritual that was once banned from being practised. The Canadian government forbade all ceremonies in an effort to kill Indigenous culture, kill Indigenous people. The tall one knows that taking part in a sundance is a solemn promise to Creator to live a good life, to cause no harm, and to work towards strengthening the culture. And, even though his own life has fallen by the wayside, he still respects the teaching, and the memory of his grandfather.

"No one that holy would ever do what you've done here today," he says, as John holds his breath. "That's right, I have a Mooshum, too, and he has scars just like yours. But he ain't no hypocrite. Mooshum told me what those marks mean." Levoy holds the gun point blank at John's temple. "You aren't good and you hurt people, you piece of shit. That's why you need to be taught a lesson. I am gonna sew your foreskin together with this needle and thread. And if you make a sound, my boy here will paste your brains all over this bedspread. You want scars? These ones you will remember. Fucker."

Levoy neglects to explain that his strong family and tradition structures fell apart after his Mooshum went to the spirit world. Too much grief and sadness about that has caused chaos ever since. No more roots. That's why Levoy takes such exception to seeing those scars on someone who clearly has no problem inflicting scars on others.

Ever so slowly, the tall one delights in inflicting each stitch. There is only the smallest amount of blood as the needle pierces. John Wayne scowls in pain but silently so. He doesn't want to get shot. Once the tall one finishes his handiwork, the men leave, carrying Purdy who is wrapped in the hotel blanket. What they leave behind is a droopy mess.

John Wayne never makes it to the education conference.

53. INNOCENCE

MAYNARD AND SHAD WALK and walk and walk for hours amongst the land at Condie Nature Refuge, a happy Misty running by their side, until the obvious question has to be asked. "You hungry?" Shad inquires.

"Kind of," Maynard says and rubs his stomach. "My Dad taught me how to make a makeshift rod. Maybe I'll throw one in and see if we can pull up some fish." Maynard neglects to mention the picnic lunch that he packed.

"I've got a better idea," Shad points towards the parking lot. "It's a bit of a drive, but worth it."

Twenty minutes later, the trio sit on the steps of the Bluebird Café. Best fish and chips in the province, according to Shad. "Geez, sorry I made you pay for my meal, Shad," Maynard offers, "but I didn't even think to bring my wallet. Never do when I head out on the land. Just a habit, I guess."

The café is located in the nearby resort community of Regina Beach located on Last Mountain Lake and alongside the land known as Kinookimaw, where Nina holds her Moon Ceremonies. The Bluebird Café has been serving up fish 'n' chips since 1928. "I come here every summer. Make the drive out, specifically for this," Shad says, squeezing some fresh lemon over his battered cod.

"What are you doing?" Maynard hasn't eaten battered fish before, only pan-friend and he never douses his with lemon.

"What do you mean?" Shad is puzzled.

"I mean, the lemon. Why would you squeeze a lemon over your fish?"

"Don't know. Just have always done it," Shad says, and tries to quell a belly laugh, thinking it a funny question.

"And, what is this?" Maynard asks, holding up the small container of tartar sauce. "It's sauce for the fish. You've never tried it before?" This time Shad can't help but let out a bit of laughter as he feeds Misty a couple of freshly-cut potato fries. "Try it," he says, "new experiences are the spice of life."

"Oh, I don't know about that," Maynard hesitates. "Back home, the only time we smother something in a sauce is when the meat is already close to going bad, but still edible. Masks the taste. We only put salt n' pepper on our fish back home."

"Oh, come on, live a little. Here." Shad opens his tartar sauce condiment package and puts a bit on his finger. He lifts it up to Maynard's lips for a taste. A small moment of intimacy that Maynard accepts. He smile upon tasting the piquant flavour. "That is good. Okay, I'll try it."

The two men eat their meal, sitting on the Rockwell-esque concrete steps of the Café and in comfortable silence watching the throngs of tourists who've also made their way to the Beach. Since running into Maynard at the Den that night, it has been Shad's plan to bring him out to the Nature Refuge and to Regina Beach. He hopes Maynard will realize that while southern Saskatchewan doesn't hold the same grandeur of landscape as the north, there is more to the south than simply flat prairie and busy cities. The Qu'Appelle Valley is a jewel. Shad senses that though Maynard is enjoying his visit down south, he is a little overwhelmed with the pace of life in the Queen City. Shad knows that Maynard grew up on the land and the largest city he's ever been to is Prince Albert. Shad thought a day trip like this might help his new friend find a comfort zone and maybe extend Maynard's visit beyond just a few days.

"If it gets too hot we can always jump in the lake. I'm sure Misty would like that too."

Maynard finds himself getting slightly aroused at the suggestion, knowing it means Shad will be required to disrobe. He glances at his new friend's muscular arms and chest and he wonders if there are tan lines underneath his clothes, especially around the pelvic area.

After their meal, the trio doesn't jump in the lake. Instead, they take a leisurely walk down the pathway that leads towards Kinookimaw and a place known as The Point. Maynard makes sure to use his disposable camera often, snapping pictures of the land and of Shad and Misty. He realizes that it is the first time since arriving this far south in the province that he is feeling relaxed and content. While hiking, Shad talks about the history of the area and how many decades ago the hills of Kinookimaw used to serve as a buffalo jump. He talks about the pathway on which they walk, which used to be the railway line. "There was a passenger train that used to run to the area. But once the train stopped, only this pathway has remained." When they reach The Point, it surprises Maynard to see a train trestle connecting both sides of Last Mountain Lake, from The Point to the Little Arm, which is the land across the way. "Don't see that often." An hour later they are standing at the trestle and Misty is frolicking in the lake. A perfect time for Maynard to suggest that they walk along the trestle and see if they can keep their balance without falling in.

"Geez. Wish we'd made this walk earlier. Can do it all another time I suppose, but look," Shad points at his watch, "getting a bit late." He reminds Maynard that he promised to cook dinner for his cousins this evening.

The delight of the day's activities caused that factor to slip from Maynard's mind, "Holy. I totally forgot. Haven't even planned anything..." He hesitates for one second. "You will join us all for dinner tonight, eh?"

"Wouldn't have it any other way, my friend."

As they make their way back to the main beach, and the parking lot where Shad's car is parked, Maynard makes a suggestion, "Think we should stop off at a grocery store in the city, if that's all right with you. I'll pay you back. But, I did tell my cousins I'd cook dinner tonight. Kind of late now, so maybe we should just pick up something quick."

Not a problem. It's been a full day. Topping it off with a good meal, even if already prepared at an in-store deli, is a good idea.

Once back in the city, they make a quick stop at the Safeway at Regina's Northgate Mall. Shad elects to go in, because he has his wallet. Maynard agrees to stay with Misty and wait in the car.

It is while waiting quietly in the parking lot that Maynard notices corn stocks across the way. They are planted in the middle of the boulevard of busy Albert Street North. Large stalks, planted as the focal point to accentuate a floral garden. And the corn is ready.

Maynard leaves Misty in the vehicle and walks across the busy intersection. He starts picking the ripe cobs.

54. WORDS UNSPOKEN TELL THE TALE

SHAD RETURNS TO THE PARKED VEHICLE, wanting to offer an apology for having taken so long to exit the grocery store. There was a huge line up at the cashier and only one lane open. But he is happy with the feast he's selected and now carries in the collection of paper bags that fill his arms. Dry ribs, BBQ ribs, pasta salad and fresh garden salad, an assortment of imported cheese, including bulbs of garlic to bake with brie, and, of course, sparkling water and pop. His excitement wanes and then turns to worry when he discovers that Maynard is not in the car. Misty is there. But no Maynard.

Shad places the items he's purchased in the trunk then does a visual sweep of the parking lot. He sees only rows and rows of parked cars, but no Maynard. He wonders if maybe his friend needed to use the washroom and went inside the mall, so decides to sit with Misty in his vehicle and wait.

He waits and waits and waits to the point of worry. It's been a half hour and it looks as though twilight promises to set in. Shad finally decides to drive. He thinks maybe Maynard has walked back to Sandy's home. The reason? There is no logic. But he has food in the trunk and a dog in the back seat needs to stretch her legs. Shad starts his ignition, puts his stylish red Toyota Camry in gear and drives south on Albert Street.

Sandy who answers the door and an excited Misty jumps into her arms. "Hi Shad, lovely day you had, I hope? So glad y'all are here. We are starving."

"Indeed, we had a wonderful day," he replies with a weak smile. "And we picked up some dinner for everyone, as promised." Shad hands her the grocery bags. "Maynard here?"

Sandy is puzzled by his question.

Just then a distraught Charlene joins her sister who is still standing in the entry way by the front door. "I just got a call from the police station. Maynard has been arrested."

Minutes later they are entering the main station of the Regina Police Service downtown, a sterile and cold building. A surly security guard questions Sandy who is the first to approach the desk "What's your business, Miss?" He is an older gentleman who looks to be weary of hearing tales of societal woes.

"I'm here to pick up my cousin. Maynard Bear. We just got a phone call from him. Says he's being held for questioning."

The security guard moves in slow motion, never meeting her eye, repeatedly checking a stack of paper files on his desk. "Oh, yes. A mischief charge. Got picked up with no ID. Have a seat Miss, I'll call down to the holding cells."

It takes another fifteen minutes before Maynard appears, in handcuffs and escorted by an officer to the front desk. Charlene rushes to hug her cousin, handing over his wallet. It contains Maynard's identification. It had been sitting on Sandy's coffee table in her living room alongside neatly stacked bedding stored under the coffee table.

"Oh my God, Maynard, what happened?" Charlene questions. It is the officer who is escorting him who answers. "Been charged with a count of public mischief, Miss. He's being released with a promise to appear in court on Monday, two weeks from now. There's some paperwork to fill out before we release him."

This? A life lesson? Who knows? And once they all arrive back home at Sandy's, who cares? Everyone is safe and accounted for.

It is the smell of a backyard campfire that greets everyone, once they finally return from the police station. Nina and Mary

Ann are still at Sandy's home and have set up some chairs and a small card table in the backyard. Misty, meantime, has set up camp underneath the table, waiting for some scraps of the feast, which has been put on hold but now promises to finally begin. The end to a very eventful day.

"Charged with mischief?" Nina asks. "What on earth did you do?"

Maynard is sheepish in reply but looks relieved, explaining that a police car picked him up while he was picking the corn cobs, "Thought they'd be great for tonight's dinner. Until they told me I was destroying public property. Charged me with mischief for picking corn."

"No! Really? You'd think they have better things to attend to," Nina replies, handing a platter of ribs to be passed around the circle of lawn chairs by the fire. Charlene, meantime, passes up the offering of food. She's lost her appetite, still sickened by her own vivid imagination and distress about what might have happened to her cousin.

When she took the phone call earlier her first worry was that Maynard had been targeted and arrested for being gay. Something that's been happening in the news stories she's been listening to on the radio lately. Something she's always suspected about Maynard. That he is different. But something that has never been said out loud. She has never asked her cousin directly. If he was to come out—holy—this is not the way to do it, she thinks. But he's home now. And safe. The way it should be.

"Were you scared being held in a cell like that?" Char holds her cousin's hand, wanting to speak about those other worries on her mind, but she can't bring herself to ask.

Maynard shakes his head, "No, not scared. More like confused. How can a person get arrested for picking corn that is growing in a public place? What? If the deer came over to eat it, they wouldn't be arrested. I still can't believe they took me in. And charged me too. I have never committed a criminal act in my life." Maynard contemplates, adding, "And to answer your question, cousin. No, not scared. Mostly because being held in a cell kind of reminded me of being in a fishing shack. Small. No real windows and I suppose there was a honey hole in there too! A chamber pot in the corner." He laughs.

"You need to be more careful in the city," Charlene adds. "It's not like back home." Misty interrupts the moment of clarity that Charlene longs to address but doesn't know how to bring up. The dog jumps on Maynard's lap, spilling his plate of food.

"Misty, you little stinker. Get down," Sandy chuckles, offering the dog a rib bone to lure her back onto the lawn. "And, oh, forgot to mention to you Maynard, John Wayne popped by today. Out of the blue. Mentioned he was hoping to take you for lunch."

"Darn. Sorry I missed him. What the heck? He's not staying here tonight?"

All four women shake their head no. But offer no explanation.

Maynard is confused about that. He's been taught that family always accepts family. While unsure about the moment, he decides to lighten the mood, and says, "But no worries. Knowing our cousin, he'll probably drop by, unannounced again, tomorrow." While picking up the food that Misty spilled, he asks, "Did he say where he is staying?"

"He didn't say." Charlene responds.

"Well, my guess is he's probably having a great time somewhere in the city tonight. He always manages to find excitement. Probably dining on lobster at some high-end restaurant and gaining support for his ideas to revamp the curriculum. Likely holding court with a bunch of Chiefs is my guess."

Maynard couldn't be more mistaken.

55. BACK AT THE SHELTER

S HE HAS TRAVELLED ALMOST A THOUSAND miles to put a space of safety between her and the man she once loved—but now fears. It is still disconcerting to Mary Ann that John Wayne showed up out of the blue earlier today. Seeing him loosened an emotional scab. Some time alone with Nina, here in the alcove of the women's shelter's backyard, just might provide the remedy she's been seeking. "Your bruises healed well," Nina says as she gently brushes Mary Ann's bangs from her eyes. "All you can do is keep living until you feel alive again, my girl." It seems the perfect moment for Nina to again mention what she saw in her vision earlier that day. That Mary Ann needs a spirit name to help protect and guide her, "I will call on my brother to help prepare for the ceremony. His name is Joe Bush Sr. "

It is not the first time Mary Ann hears the name. She remembers hearing it when Sandy came to visit Gabriel's cabin. Nina adds, "I was Joe's apprentice, several years ago. We met at his niece's pow wow initiation out at Whitecap. She's a fancy dancer." She talks about how Joe was the one who gifted her with a pipe. "'*We need more women back leading the Circle*,' he told me. He is the one who held my own naming ceremony. He told me my spirit name. Kaskiti Maskwas Iskwiw, Black Bear Woman.

"We held a ceremony, too. That is the way it is supposed to be done," Nina says. "Honest to goodness, since carrying my name and my pipe, I've met people out there who have offered me money, asking if they can buy a name. Like you can just pick one up at the corner store. Holy. I always decline when they ask that way. They don't even know to offer tobacco." Nina gives a useful piece of advice to Mary Ann who may someday be her young apprentice. "Always be aware of the charlatans, my girl. Like if someone asks you for money in order to conduct ceremony. I've met people who need money for beer or smokes and they offer to sell a blessing for cash. Or if they require you to give them money in order to receive your name. Get out fast."

"No!" Mary Ann is dismayed.

"Oh, yes. I always say: if it doesn't feel right then it probably is not right. So don't do it and don't believe everything you hear."

Nina remembers another example. "I even met someone at the shelter this past year who refused to use toothpaste. Was told it was a way of protecting herself."

"I don't follow," Mary Ann is intent on hearing more details.

"Yes," Nina continues. "The client said she went to see someone who advertised as a healer. She'd been having trouble sleeping, so he told her to stop using toothpaste because he believed that fluoride calcifies the third eye, and that's why she was out of balance. Can you believe it?" Nina takes a sip of water. "She didn't even know what the third eye meant but before leaving, she paid him thirty dollars for that bogus information."

She pauses for another moment, and recalls another example. "And I was so sad to hear about another time. A couple who had just recently separated but had hopes for reconciliation. Until the person, like John Wayne, told that man *'Never wish to be reunited or to heal that relationship. It brings bad luck.'* He went on to tell a story about how wishing for a renewal of love leads to death and that if he is reunited with his wife he would face death and so would his daughter. Feeding his fears. Turns out that all along what this phony wanted was to set up this man with his own sister and figured if the ex-wife wasn't in the picture, it would be easier to orchestrate. And he used his position to do this. But what kind of relationship can be based on fear? And those two never did get back together."

"And, what kind of person leaves someone without hope?" Mary Ann asks.

"Someone with another agenda, that's who," Nina replies. "Like I said, if it doesn't feel right, then it isn't. We need to use common sense and ask questions. That's allowed."

Mary Ann's body language indicates she is visibly more at ease, sitting here in the shelter of an alcove, the last rays of the day's sun warming her skin. "I guess I need to wipe my memory clean."

Nina cautions that there are no hard and fast rules as to who might be authentically called and gifted in the spiritual realm. "I have to also say that I have met many who were so lost and destructive. Even Joe Bush was one of them, once, a long time ago. But love turned his life around, in the truest sense of the word. Love of life. Love of culture. And we are all blessed that people like him finally embraced his calling. People who are now respected Elders who accept their role with reverence and wisdom. Who lead our people back to where we are supposed to be, without expecting some sort of payment." She collects her thoughts, then adds, "But there are those who are still ruled by fear and ego, and it is easier to hate than to love. It is easier to run away and blame others rather than to face your fears or to admit your own shortcomings. So they do things or say things to keep you doubting yourself. That's why they give you false information, like the man who broke up that family."

Fitting that Nina would end with this thought just as Grand-mother Moon begins to rise again. "Inner wisdom, my child. It's what you need to rely upon, too. Spirit surrounds you always, especially in times of darkness. They will protect you."

She hugs her young protégé and says a prayer that Mary

Ann understands everthing that she has just shared. And she does discern that her grieving for John is more for what should have been, or what she had hoped it to be, instead of what it really was.

56. ROBERTA REMEMBERS

BY ITS VERY NATURE, it's often believed that small talk is trivial. It can be. But at other times it is ripe with fond memory. Such is the case this noon hour, as Roberta enjoys her last bite of sandwich. She still lives in her dad's little cabin in the woods.

Inspired by a conversation while out fishing with her cousin yesterday, Roberta harvested fresh lettuce and tomatoes from her small backyard garden early this morning. Her dad built the raised garden for her in early spring. Because there are so many wild rabbits, raccoons, and deer roaming the woods near the cabin, Murray also constructed an enclosed space using leftover boards from his old fishing boat that sprung a leak a couple of years ago. Over the top of the structure wire mesh keeps the varmints out but lets the sunshine in. And it's worked like a charm.

"What's your favourite comfort food?" Roberta's cousin, Rita, had asked.

"I can't answer that question, Rita," Roberta replied. "I find it depends on my mood. Or the weather outside. Or even the season." They've been having small talk conversations like this their entire lives. Because Rita used to live just up the road, it was customary for the child Roberta to jump on her bike and spend sunrise to sunset outdoors playing with her cousin.

Like her, Roberta is happy Rita's come home for the summer. In part, Rita came back to spend time with her own aging father whose health has been questionable since last winter. Rita is trained in something called Reiki and essential oils, which she thinks will help her dad in his healing. Roberta understands neither and asks no questions. She's just glad for the company and for the familiarity.

To Roberta, Rita's dad is simply called *Uncle*, even though his first name is Matthew. He's a couple of years younger than her dad, Murray, although the two could be twins in both appearance and mannerisms. They have been hunting together, laughing together, and fishing together since they were boys. Everything is so very familiar. Which is why everyone was so surprised when Matthew injured himself.

His ice fishing shack is like a second home during the winter seasons. But for some reason, Matthew didn't take his own advice one afternoon and didn't wear the proper footwear: heavy Sorels with plenty of grip. Even he was shocked to have slipped on the ice and broken his leg. Murray took him in and brother Matty stayed at his cabin for several weeks. But his injury never healed properly and some phantom pain is still bothering him. That's why Rita has come home for the summer. To nurse her dad back to good health using alternative remedies. Calling on spirit and the land to provide good health. It couldn't have made Roberta happier to be hanging with her cousin again.

Their afternoon conversation the day before reminds Roberta about family, food, and familiarity. And that causes nostalgia, with Roberta longing to ingest happy memory. So today, it is a fresh lettuce and tomato sandwich, served on white bread with a dollop of Miracle Whip and sprinkled with salt and pepper. The exact same way her mom, Grace, used to make it.

Yesterday's visit was good medicine.

Roberta has been feeling more at peace these past months, here in the solitude of the northern bush. The place where she grew up. A life unconcerned with the outside world, that is until she takes an empty bottle of orange juice to the recycle bin. The empties are kept back behind the wood shed -and that is where she spies some lettering on an empty beer can. A source of shame. She had buried those beer cans under all the other juice and pop containers months ago. Can't hide them elsewhere because there is no recycling depot nearby and a recycling load is taken to the city only once a year. The money from it is used to stock up on flour, spices, and lard.

Upon seeing the beer can, an even deeper sense of shame overcomes her. Maybe it has been her clean living, or being out here in nature every day. Maybe it's because she has been lucid and sober for months, except for that one slip. As she holds the empty beer can in her hand, something seems to nudge Roberta. Somehow, and most vividly, it is almost as though she is having a vision, and recalling that dark night that John Wayne visited when her dad was away hunting. She hadn't drunk alcohol for weeks leading up to that night, and she hasn't had any since. Well, except for the beers he left in the fridge, the empties now hidden under this pile of recyclable material.

She's mentioned that evening to no one. And she finds herself thankful that John Wayne hasn't come around to the cabin since.

Spoke to soon.

Because during this moment of safe thoughts in a safe place, Roberta sees John Wayne's black truck moving quickly along the grid road. It fills her with a sense of dread that she can't put her finger on.

So Roberta begins to scratch absentmindedly around the crotch area of the ripped jeans she's wearing. It occurs to her that she's been doing a lot of that these past months. Itching and scratching. And she smells different now when she wipes herself after urinating. She worries that she may be suffering from a vaginal infection of sorts, but how is it possible? She hasn't been intimate with anyone since leaving the south and moving back in with her dad.

She decides it is worth getting checked. Roberta goes back

in to the cabin to check an article she recently saw in the local newspaper. It was an ad listing the times, dates, and places where northern community health clinics are being held in the coming days.

57. CAN'T HIDE FROM SPIRIT

S UMMER MEMORIES ARE QUICKLY REPLACED by the splendour of colour in autumn. Which just as fast turns to ice and snow. John Wayne has been laying low for months now. And no one seems to miss him.

He's bundled up for the frigid cold today, as he checks the snares he's set near his cabin. Nothing. It's been like this for weeks and so odd. He knows there are rabbits in the area. Sees their tracks, running long strides ahead of the fox prints that follow. No rabbits means he will have another meal of spam and eggs fried in lard again today. He won't make another attempt at baking bannock. That too has been off. Seems no matter how much baking powder he adds, the bread comes out flat. His bannock won't rise.

He is spooked by a sudden noise coming from the brush up ahead. He checks the ground, now covered with just the slightest bit of snowfall. No markings. His instinct warns of danger until he spies a red cardinal perched on a jack pine in the clearing he's headed towards.

His edge softens, remembering a story told by his mother several years ago.

They were out picking blueberries. Little Johnny must have been no older than eight years old.

"Nikawiy, kiwapamitin ekwa e-kaskeyimitan." John's own mother says, to a bird perched high above.

"Who do you miss, Mama?" The small boy asks, interpreting from the Cree words she's just spoken.

John's parents, while fluent, have been insisting their little Johnny speak in English.

John's mom remembers only too well, and painfully, how she was slapped with a ruler in the residential school anytime her language was used.

"Kohkum," Johnny remembers his mom's reply, "that's her right there." She points to the colourful bird. "Kohkum told me, a long time ago, that when you see a Cardinal it is a sign that someone who loves you is visiting from the spirit world."

She ruffles his hair and smiles, "Anytime you see one, say a prayer and leave some tobacco."

It's as though she had spoken just moments ago. John fetches an ever-present pouch of tobacco from his front jacket pocket. "Nikawiy, kiwapamitin ekwa e-kaskeyimitan." Mama, I see you and I miss you, he repeats in the Cree language before laying a sprinkling of tobacco on the ground. His moment of closeness interrupted, he surveys the tire marks in the snow. They lead to his driveway.

It is with a sense of relief when he arrives at his door that he finds Stan waiting there. Otherwise known as Eskab ay wiss and John Wayne's helper in preparing for ceremony. He's been waiting for months to receive some kind of direction. "My nephew is sick," he admits. "Do you think maybe it's time to rebuild the sweat?" Eskab ay wiss never mentions John's short hair. Figures John will share with him in his own time why he cut off his braid. Never knowing, of course, that John didn't cut his hair. It was an act of violence that took his hair, like so many other things in John's life.

John hasn't been holding himself up as spiritual wisdom leader for some time, since returning north. He tries to cushion his absence of faith by placing blame on cousins Charlene and Sandy who questioned his authority and knowledge. And that old woman. He doesn't even remember her name. But he remembers her face. What's more he still hears the echo of her words, which in his heart he knows are words of truth.

"You? Live in a place of fear, which you call faith. You believe it will erase what you have done and continue to do. Nothing can be undone until you admit your doing. I have gone through so much. We all have, and we have earned a place of courage. You? You still live in a place of fear. But praying is not enough. Until you admit your wrongdoing and make amends."

They are words that haunt him, mostly at night while he's tossing and trying to get some rest. He wonders how that woman could even say such things. She doesn't know anything about him.

Or perhaps she knows everything about him. That's his fear.

It's caused him many times to rub his forehead. It's where he has a deep scar just above his left eyebrow. An accident that happened when he was a toddler.

John is the youngest of three. No one says it, but his birth was not planned. He knows this because both of his brothers were already sent away to attend high school in the city by the time he was born. To this day, he's not very close to either of them. Both his parents died some time ago. He remembers they drank a lot when he was very little, often leaving him alone. They had stopped drinking by the time John Wayne became a teenager. But, as a child and even through his parents' addictions, John was never really alone. John remembers having several invisible playmates who would follow him everywhere. To him, they were as real as the family dog, who also followed him around. John got the scar after an accident in the bush one summer afternoon. He was maybe three. Maybe four.

He remembers.

His parents had again been drinking and were both passed out, naked, on makeshift wooden furniture out on the veranda. That furniture is still on the deck.

Little Johnny was hungry, but as there was no food in the house he wandered out into the bush by himself. He'd done it before with his mom. Gone into the bush to pick berries. But this time, he wandered too far and got lost. But he wasn't afraid. Those little people followed him and made sure he was safe. Even so, they couldn't stop him from slipping on a river rock and hitting his head. It must have been a heck of a fall to leave a gash and a scar he's carried his whole life. He doesn't remember getting home but still remembers being gently removed from the water before he drowned. He recalls being carried through the woods by a man with a rack of horns like an elk. When he woke up, little Johnny was laying on the veranda of his home. A mixture of clay and ferns were now dried on his forehead. Something to stop the bleeding. His parents didn't even notice that he was gone. His mother woke up later in the afternoon. Stumbled to the kitchen and made her boy some boiled rice with raisins. To this day, he doesn't know if the man with horns was real or simply in his imagination. It's all he remembers. But he's still alive, perhaps destined for something grand?

Eskab ay wiss understands John Wayne has gone to a place of deep reflection again. John Wayne has been quiet and keeping to himself lately. Eskab ay wiss won't pry and decides to cut his visit short but not before handing John a package of tobacco, "Just got it at the gas station. Thought I'd ask you about rebuilding the sweat lodge and let you know I am here to help anytime." Before he turns to leave, Eskab ay wiss says something that puts a fear in John.

"Have the RCMP been here?"

Desperate eyes come from those who lie. And it's a look John cannot cover up when he responds. "No. Why?"

"I ran into that young Corporal just now when I was filling my tank."

"What did he want?" John attempts to mask a look of worry.

"It was the strangest question. About the sweat lodge," Eskab ay wiss searches his memory. "He wanted to know if we are clothed or naked when we conduct ceremony. And whether there is any physical touching as part of the ceremony. Made me uncomfortable. Don't you think that's weird?"

"Weird. Yes." John is unnerved. "Why'd he want to know something like that?"

"No idea. But I did notice him pulling into Old Murray's driveway too when I was coming over here." Eskab ay wiss surmises, "Maybe they just wanted to talk to him about poachers. There's been a lot of that happening lately. And Old Murray knows the land better than anyone. Who knows? But I do remember Murray mentioning something about odd tracks he'd seen in the snow last time he was out on the land."

Poachers?

Probably not.

58. NOVEMBER KASKATINOWIPISIM

"SIX DEGREES OF SEPARATION IN ACTION," Sandy exclaims and can hardly contain her glee, rushing to the curbside when she sees Joe Bush Sr. and Amos pull up in front of her home. She doesn't even give Joe a chance to open the passenger side door, pulling the handle open before Amos even has the chance to change the gear from drive to park. She squeals, "Joe! Oh, so great to see you! Quick! Undo your seatbelt so I can give you a hug."

The Old Man is just as happy to see Sandy, "My daughter," he gives her a bear hug, "you look so happy."

"Happier now that you're here."

By now, Amos has joined them. He has traditionally-adopted Sandy as his sister, "Dad. It's my turn," he hugs her as well.

"Oh. How I have missed you both since moving back to Regina. Come," Sandy motions, "everyone is waiting inside. And, holy, we have been waiting so long for you to come visit. We made some food."

They have been waiting months for a reunion.

For people like Joe, there really is no such thing as retirement. The reason he hasn't been able to show up for Mary Ann's naming ceremony until now is because he feels he cannot say no. The traditional ways have been lost in too many cases, been hidden in others. Knowledge keepers, the real ones, are precious and in high demand. People need to spend time with them. People long to spend time with them. It's why Joe and

Amos have been travelling. All across the province of Ontario for weeks, waking up spirit within, and reminding Indigenous people of the beauty we possess, and that was almost taken from us. Almost lost.

Mother Earth needs our love. It's real. Spirit is alive and guides us. It's real. Magic is afoot. It's real.

Almost taken, like our children, but the knowledge is sacred and has been spared. Didn't die although many have tried. But you can't kill spirit. It's alive. Joe and Amos have been the sentinels, watching, guiding, and illuminating those who are open, those who wish to remember. Now he's back home in Saskatchewan and sitting with another he's helped bring to life through Indigenous traditional teachings. Sandy.

Joe knows Sandy has seen Centaur. It came to him in a dream and he reassures Sandy not to be afraid. "You've been learning. He just shows up once in a while to check in and make sure you are keeping on track." He points to Misty, and says, "And the Little People are back in your life too. Maybe this little one right here," he pats Misty's head, "is one of them."

Joe tells her a story about how sometimes the Little People, who are usually invisible, get so attached to the person they are protecting that they ask Creator for magic. To transform them into another shape, so that they can interact on a real basis with the people they love. "My guess is, sometimes you think of Misty as more like a person than a dog?"

"Yes," Sandy replies, "like she knows things and how to respond in ways that make me feel better, if I am sad as an example. But, honestly Joe, I haven't been sad for such a long time. Can't remember the last time. Ever since Charlene moved in I just feel happy." But then a bit of sadness creeps in. "But, I do have to admit that there are times, mostly when we go on long walks with Misty and Char tells me stories about Nikawiy, our mom, that I feel sorrow. So many years lost. I should have grown up with my sister and experienced the stories instead of just hearing them now."

"You can't think like that, Sandy," Joe says. "You need to concentrate on the blessing that she's a part of your life now. You'll have memories and new experiences and learn together," He points to a small table that's been set up in Sandy's living room. "I see you have started sewing."

Sandy feels it is the right time to get the item she's made for Joe. She's sewn him a medicine bag similar to the one Nina always carries. "It's the colours of the first star blanket you and Amos gave me when we first met." She points to the star blanket hanging on the wall. "It's sacred to me, that blanket. And a reminder that I never walk alone."

Sandy explains that she never had an interest in learning to sew until she had a vision one night. "It came in a dream. That's when I asked Nina to teach me how to sew. The dream also told me to make a jingle dress for my little sister."

"But you don't have a little sister." Joe says. "Oh, but I do." Sandy tells Joe the story of little Betsy. A ward of the state who showed up in the home in which Sandy grew up. The little girl was four years old. Sandy was nine. "I loved her so much, Joe." Sandy wipes a tear, "And they took her away. Just like they took me away." Sandy says it's difficult to call her Mary Ann now that they are together again; Mary Ann and not Betsy. "But I think that would be too much for her right now, to call her Betsy. Although the name has slipped out a couple of times."

"Another time," Joe agrees. "It's delicate. And that discussion will present itself when it is supposed to. Just be thankful Creator brought the two of you together again. A blessing for the both of you." Joe. So wise. Knowing there is pain in moving forward. And that it has its own pace. Like her relationship with Charlene, Sandy knows, she and Mary Ann can start anew.

Joe Bush then tells her it's important for her to learn from women, even though he was her first teacher. "Balance, my girl. I am so proud of you. Good that you are strengthening ties with your biological family."

"Not just ties," Sandy smiles, and adds a phrase in Cree, "Mistahi kimiyototawin, nohtawiy. Kinanaskomitin ekwa kisakihithin." You have done lots for me, my father. I thank you and I love you. She has been learning Cree, which isn't so difficult considering Charlene is a fluent speaker who is always patient, ever willing and grateful that her sister is embracing the language. In return, Sandy introduced Char to Nina and now to Joe. It's taken Sandy a while to understand that rebuilding and strengthening culture happens one person at a time. And in this case, it starts with her.

"I know we have to join the others soon, nohtawiy, but before we do. I have something to ask. And, I even brought some tobacco."

Joe smiles, remembering that when Sandy first started asking questions, shortly after they first met, she never offered tobacco. Just went ahead with the questions. He didn't mind. Always said family doesn't need to offer tobacco. But, this time, Sandy insists. "Someone told me not that long ago that only certain people are allowed to pick medicines. Like sage. Is this true?"

"Oh my girl. Does it sound right to you?" Sandy doesn't answer as Joe continues, "Mother Earth provides for us all. It's like telling someone they aren't allowed to pick berries, or carrots, or rhubarb. If the medicines are being used to personally provide guidance and enlightenment anyone can pick. There may be women's protocols to be aware of. But for that information, you can talk to Nina."

As if on cue, Nina enters the room. "Okay, you two," she chuckles. "Your trip down memory road has come to an end." She hugs Joe Bush Sr. "So good to see you again, my friend. But Amos and Char and Mary Ann and I have been sipping wihkaskwapoy long enough. It's time to eat." She's wearing an apron that she brought from home and smiles at Sandy, knowing these moments alone with Joe were absolutely necessary.

59. FULL MOON FILLED WITH LOVE

SUNDAY, NOVEMBER 16. Grandmother Moon shines her delight on a new one. As magical as a wedding vow, promising to give only love to the Circle and offer beauty to the world.

Mary Ann is radiant. Thought she might be afraid. But wearing a ribbon dress made by her sister, Sandy, she feels it more protective than any plate armour worn by knights of medieval times. It is because the dress is stitched by love. The main bold colour—yellow—symbolizes new beginnings, with ribbons the colours of the earth. And red, for passion, the passion of life.

Earlier, in conversation with Nina, Joe had suggested that the ceremony happen in a sweat lodge. The place he asks the spirit world to reveal a name.

"Not a good idea right now," Nina suggests, "it will take time for Mary Ann to embrace that."

"Why?" Joe doesn't understand.

"She's afraid of the dark. And she still equates the sweat lodge with that man she used to live with. We need to respect that and give her time to realize there is nothing about spirit that needs to be feared. But that's her own walk."

So it is a Full Moon Ceremony on the land. This is the way Mary Ann is introduced to her culture, traditions, and spirituality. A place she feels safe.

Amos and Maynard have spent the afternoon gathering firewood. And Amos has gathered rocks from the water's edge as well: the Grandfathers, who will also attend tonight.

Maynard has been away for some weeks now. He had gone back up north but made the long trip south yesterday. Wouldn't miss the naming ceremony and secretly has desires that he will be receiving a spirit name as well. He's brought some fish and even some wild meat that he managed to hunt and prepare on his own. It wasn't easy for him to gut and skin and quarter this moose without the ever-watchful instruction of Old Gabriel. Not that going through the motions were difficult. He's been skilled at that since youth. It was going through the emotion of missing his dad beside him that was hard. Again, a moment of reflection. Maynard hopes his mom and dad are somehow able to be with him and his cousins tonight. Maybe his dad will arrive as an owl or as some other creature who watches over their safety during the night. But even if nothing shows itself, Maynard knows his dad will be present in spirit.

Maynard has had Old Gabriel's lucky fishhook fashioned into an earring which he wears proudly. The perfect accompaniment to his new braid, which seems to have grown longer since he's been back up north and eating the familiar diet of food from the land. Shad is the one who fashioned the fishhook into a piece of jewellery. Shad is a gifted silversmith. It's his own family tradition, which he learned from his Danish granddad. Shad's been living with Maynard in the cabin. When he first agreed to go north, the plan was that Shad would stay at his family cabin on Deschambault Lake. Wapawikoscikanik, but no longer the narrows of fear for either of them. Free to express their love, brotherhood, and friendship openly and in a sacred space that is finally fully safe for Maynard.

He's had his own insights, which came to him in the form of dreams at night. Old Gabriel smiling and telling Maynard he is proud of his son. Two-spirited. A gift that allows him to restore the balance between male and female. Like the teaching of Centaur. The bow is female symbol. The arrow is male symbol. The Centaur represents human balance.

And balance and clarity there is. Maynard never did have

to waste time on court proceedings and a possible criminal record for causing mischief. Cousin Charlene saw to that by calling one of her husband's former colleagues. A lawyer who took the role as junior partner after William's accident and death, "Call me anytime," she promised. "Anything you need." Crystal Baker made good on that promise. Taking on the case of Maynard's mischief charge at no charge and seeing that the charges were dismissed. Thrown out because the judge called the case frivolous.

Through it all, the one thing Maynard didn't win was Sandy's blessing. He had insisted that he and Shad be allowed to take Misty with them up north. "She'll only be gone for a few weeks. And she loved running through our northern pines when you visited. Please. It's only a visit and we'll take extra special good care of her." His appeal.

Sandy said no.

The naming ceremony starts by feeding the fire. More than just a phrase. Saying prayers for Mary Ann, asking that she receive guidance throughout the rest of her life, and making a food offering to those in the spirit world. Mary Ann gives Joe some broad cloth in four differing colours: red, black, white, and yellow. In doing so, she is promising to work towards bringing harmony and build bridges for each of the races on Mother Earth.

Nina facilitates the purification rites, offering the bowl of smudge to everyone present. The four sacred plants are mixed together: tobacco, cedar, sweetgrass, and sage. In tonight's ceremony, the sweetgrass used was picked by Maynard and Shad during their walk at the Condie Nature Rescue. The sage was picked right here in Kinookimaw by Sandy and Charlene.

"Nimihiowi Kakakiw Iskwew," Joe announces. "Our sister who flies high in the sky, averting danger through the use of humour and love." Dancing Raven Woman. Sandy lets go a chortle. A guttural/throat sound that is often associated with a charge to war. Nina sounds the drum she holds. "But," Joe adds, "we are not finished. We have another."

Ayikis-maskihkiy Mistanaskowew Iyiniw, Frog Medicine Badger Man is the name he gives to Maynard. It signifies the amphibian who lives in both land and water and the animal totem representing perseverance.

All the while, the fire dances and the flames take the form of The Little People in celebration. Centaur looks on from a distance. Both Joe and Nina know he is with them. They can feel it.

A light skiff of snow—large, glorious flakes begins to fall.

60. DANCING RAVEN WOMAN

ONCE BACK AT THE WOMEN'S SHELTER, Nina finally talks about significance of the ribbon skirt and why Native women wear them when rejoicing in ceremony. She tells Mary Ann that, "The bottom of your skirt touches Mother Earth and lets her know who is making their presence as she walks." She hands over a purple skirt with multi-coloured ribbons to Mary Ann. "This is my gift to you. Each time you wear it, remember who you have become. Nimihiowi Kakakiw Iskwew. The time has come for you to learn to dance."

Mary Ann is elated and rejoices in honouring her name. Yes, she decides, it is now her role to encourage others to dance. "I need to start over," she tells Nina, "and it has to start with moving away from pain. I can't live at the shelter anymore. I have been safe here but I know it's time to move forward. Can I move in with you?"

Nina already knew that Mary Ann would make the suggestion. "I have already put clean sheets on the bed in my spare room, my girl. Come," she holds out her hand, "we'll move in spirit together."

Some things are already written in the stars, things of which few have the knowledge to remember and recognize. Mary Ann doesn't need to pack up her things from the shelter. She came with nothing. But she leaves with much.

Over breakfast the next morning, Nina has already made coffee. She is wearing a new apron that has big red strawberries all over it. Strawberry teachings represent the sweetness of life. The strawberry is also called the heart berry by some, because Creator designed this little heart-shaped berry in a way that connects all of its growing functions from leaves to seeds to root just as the heart of humans connects all life within. "You like cinnamon toast?" she asks Mary Ann.

"Of course. Who doesn't?"

"Wonderful. I'll make some. Enjoy your coffee. Creamer is in the fridge." But, Nina doesn't have on her reading glasses when she goes to the pantry to retrieve the spice that always reminds her of Thanksgiving. She grabs the nearest spice container, where the powder is a deep rust colour.

After buttering the warm toast, Nina asks, "You like lots of sugar sprinkled on? Or just a bit?"

"Just a bit, thanks."

Nina tells her a nice story about how cinnamon toast always reminds her of home, and when she'd sit and listen to the stories of her Kohkum. Mary Ann feels like that now, sitting at a kitchen table with an Elder, talking about memories and how the flavours of food bring comfort until she takes a bite of the toast.

"Oh, no!" Mary Ann spits out the piece of bread on her plate.

"Excuse me?" A perplexed Nina is visibly displeased.

"Sorry, Nina. But there is something wrong with this toast." Mary Ann realizes she may have offended the Old Woman.

"What do you mean it's wrong? There is no wrong way to make cinnamon toast."

The awkward silence is broken when Mary Ann lets out a roar of laughter so hard she almost falls off her chair.

"What? Child! Have you lost it?" It takes Mary Ann another minute to regain her composure before going to the counter where Nina has left the small bottle of spice. She holds it up. "It's cayenne pepper, Nina!" She keeps giggling. "Same colour as cinnamon, I suppose, but in no way does it taste the same."

Nina should have worn her reading glasses.

Topping off their breakfast with hearty laughter, the best way to start any day.

Still giggling, Mary Ann offers to remake some real cinnamon toast. While she's at the kitchen counter and fumbling with the wire twist on the plastic bread bag, Nina starts digging through the cloth bag that holds all of the items she uses for teaching. She moves a thick braid of sweetgrass and a package of tobacco to the side, making way for her to find what she's looking for: a slim, hand-carved wooden box. It's ornate and has the design of an eagle feather carved on the cover. Inside is an eagle feather. A large flight feather that Nina took the time to elaborately bead along the bottom and to which she attached a couple of leather tassels.

It takes only a minute for the toast to reach perfect brownness. Still hot after popping up, Mary Ann slathers creamy butter and sprinkles the bread with cinnamon and sugar. No cayenne pepper this time. As she sets the plate of the fragrant toast in front of Nina, Nina slides the wooden box towards Mary Ann.

"What's this?" Mary Ann smiles.

"It's yours, my girl," Nina replies. "Go ahead. Open it."

Mary Ann lets out a small but joyful gasp as she gazes at the eagle feather contained in the box. "Oh my Lord, Nina, this is beautiful!" She gently removes the feather from the box. "No one has ever given me something so meaningful."

"You have earned it," Nina replies. "It is the same feather that was given to me years ago when I first started to dance. But now that I dance Old Style and I no longer wear feathers and beadwork, just cloth and leather and quillwork, I want you to have this, Mary Ann. Think of it as a blessing and as a sign that you, indeed, are absolutely supposed to be dancing. Wear it with pride, Nimihiowi Kakakiw Iskwew."

61. TREMBLE AND BE TROUBLED

HE ALWAYS LOVED THE QUIET of the northern bush, except for these days. Now, John Wayne finds it eerie. He's in back behind his cabin, tightening some wires for another snare. It snowed last night, and has started out as a cold morning. John is bundled up. He never takes off his black and green-striped Arctic Cat toque these days. That toque was thrown in as some bling to say, thanks for buying our product. But that company went bankrupt. Parodies. He knows he is morally bankrupt and now wears the toque to hide his shame. He is haunted each night about the sound he remembers: the flick of his own sharp hunting knife. Slicing off his identity and his pride.

He hears the sound of a vehicle approaching but there is no need for him to go to the front of the house to look and see who might be there. He knows it is not Eskab ay wiss, whose old pick-up needs a new muffler. Can hear that truck from a mile away.

Desperate acts come from those who lack.

John Wayne realizes whoever is approaching his front door will know he is in the backyard. Tell-tale footprints in fresh snow are the guide. He's been expecting the RCMP to make a visit ever since Eskab ay wiss mentioned they'd questioned him. And, ever since Eskab ay wiss talked about the police turning into his neighbour's driveway. Figures they were likely there to chat with Roberta.

She remembers? How is that possible?

And how does John Wayne know this would be the reason for a visit from police?

It's because he's had a recurring dream. More like a nightmare that shakes him from slumber. In that dream, Roberta opens her blood shot eyes and removes the clothes pin from her nipple.

Guilt prompts him into guessing. She remembers. He worries that others might know by now, too. Maybe some type of whisper campaign in the community? No one has come to visit him in weeks except for Eskab ay wiss.

He worries because he passed Roberta on the grid road the other day. She didn't smile and wave, like she's always done since getting her driver's licence just a couple of years ago. She didn't even meet his glance as he passed.

A hard knock at the door, in the distance. John Wayne hears two voices in conversation.

"Maybe he's out checking his traps."

"Should we get the dog?" the second voice questions.

"No need. Fresh snow today. We can just follow his tracks."

John hears their footsteps returning to the vehicle. He hears a vehicle door open and close. Figures they've likely gone for their weapons. Shotguns.

He drops the axe he's holding and runs towards the bush. He knows hiding places, hidden trails, the way out. He's been roaming these woods all his life. Knows the gullies and places where his footprints will disappear. Tracking game. Knows how to make sure no one tracks him. He touches his hunting knife that he's been keeping close since returning from the city. No one has called him since that day.

Except for Eskab ay wiss no one has visited either. Not even Maynard, who John Wayne knows has returned back up north. He caught a glimpse of him and some other guy the other day at the gas bar. Cousin. Why doesn't anyone look in on him? Does he even want them to?

John begins to pour sweat, removing his toque and jamming

it into the pocket of his downy parka. The coat is the colour of camouflage that will stick out this time of year when all that surrounds is white—bereft of colour, like his own world has become.

By now, he's deep in the bush and surrounded by only the sounds of silence. He's at a creek. One that feeds the Puskwakau River. The small trickle of open water is his escape. A way of losing his tracks.

He'll head towards Wapawikoscikanik, the narrows of fear. A place of ambush. And there he will wait. It's here, hiding in a snow-covered bluff, that John Wayne hears the voice of that old woman again. *You can fool people. But you can never hide from spirit*

And it is then that John notices he is not alone. And that it isn't the police who've found him.

He sees a set of cloven hoof marks. And doesn't need to wonder to whom they belong.

John Wayne can only take a guess at what that might mean. He remembers the stories his Mooshum told about the Bushman. And never to look back if you hear someone following you in the bush. John can only think that this time—if it is the man with large antlers—he is not likely there to pick John Wayne up in protective arms. Nor likely to carry him back to the safety of his veranda.

John concedes. Lays his hunting knife down in the snow and falls to his knees.

You can't hide from spirit.

No one hears from John Wayne after that day. His disappearance is noted. But his body is never found.

62. GATHERING OF NATIONS

"Geez, Maynard," Sandy snickers in jest, "how many sandwiches do we need? Sheesh. You've packed enough for an army."

"It's a long trip," Maynard replies, "no gas station cardboard sandwiches for you, my lovely cousin."

It started out as just an idea last fall. To drive to Albuquerque, New Mexico. And today, they are all heading to the Gathering of Nations. The world's biggest pow wow, held every April.

Maynard and Shad arrived from up north just yesterday bringing gifts of whitefish, neckbones, and moose ribs and roasts. Plus, some leg bones for Misty to chew on.

"I will be your co-pilot," he says to Sandy, "because I am the only one who remembered to buy a map."

"Well, maybe you bought the map but I am still riding shot gun," Charlene tells him. She pops in a cassette tape of fiddle tunes. "Boil Them Cabbage Down" is a fiddle song that provides lively background music for spirited conversation.

They have rented a large passenger van. There is no room in Sandy's Jeep for six people. Mary Ann, herself, Charlene, Amos (who has been a grass dancer for years), Shad, and Maynard each look forward to the trip.

They are at the highway junction near Milestone, Saskatchewan, when Sandy reveals a plan. She is pondering leaving her career as a journalist and going into clothing design. "You have a degree in Business Administration, Maynard, maybe you can help me get started. Maybe I will even open a shop. Imagine that, me—an entrepreneur? I've always dreamed of having a place where people can go that supports our local artisans. No 'Made in China' stickers anywhere. Everything is genuinely hand-crafted and authentic. I think there is a need."

"For you, my love, anything," Maynard smiles.

Sandy also says she is considering buying the house in which she lives, "Feels like home ever since Charlene decided to stay with me in the city."

New beginnings. It's never been Char's plan to leave the north for good. And she won't. She travels back to her family home—a cabin in the woods—anytime she needs a spiritual recharge with the land and memory. It's surprising even to her that the pace of the city is what has helped her drown out the noise that silence can leave. Too much time alone by herself up north. Too much time to think about what was, instead of what is. She's been hired at the shelter, full time as a counsellor and medical professional. It keeps her immersed in the community she's built, which includes prayer, smudging, ribbon skirts, and friendship. And, she's started her own dance troupe. Weekly lessons on how to jig. She is sharing what she loves and introduces things that are rich about the north to this city. There is sewing involved, too. Flouncy skirts held up by stiff crinoline and satin blouses with puffy sleeves. It's something she and Sandy often work on. The kitchen table in their home now resembles Nina's. A place no longer designed simply for dining, now a place for creating memories.

Sandy, in the meantime, has also finally started taking piano lessons. Doesn't make sense to have such a lovely instrument in her home but never hear its voice. Fiddle next? And maybe even jigging.

Maynard will miss his cousin, but knows he can visit anytime. It is a scenic and reflective drive from north to south. Besides, Shad's family lives in Regina, so regular trips to the south are definitely on the agenda. He smiles and offers some advice.

"Good idea, cuz," he says. "I think we should all make a list of things we wish to do. But instead of calling it a bucket list, we should call it a 'fuck it' list."

Charlene laughs so hard it causes her to spray the wihkask-wapoy tea she's sipping across the dashboard. "Maynard! Language please. This is a grown-up van, you know."

"Speaking of which," Sandy pipes in. "There is a gift for you in that shopping bag under your seat, Maynard."

He reaches for the bag that makes a clinking sound as he moves it to his lap. "Oh my gawd. Awww. This is beautiful." Maynard removes a stunning red and white jingle dress, "You made this for me?"

"I did so. But, it was actually Amos's idea."

This isn't Amos's first rodeo; he's made the trip to Albuquerque many times. "There is likely to be a switch dance," Amos says and tries to explain why Sandy made him a dress.

"What's that? A switch dance?" Shad inquires.

Amos explains that while pow wows are a celebration of culture, there is also plenty of room for laughter and fun too. A switch dance is when men are invited to dress up in women's regalia and the women wear a man's dance outfit. "They dance each others' dance. And there is a lot of misstepping, even more laughter, and I suppose maybe it's a way of saying there's a bit of switch in each of us. It's important to honour both the feminine and the masculine, even in an unconventional way."

Amos' explanation gives them a sense of tranquility and acceptance, which is really what this road trip is all about.

"There's a gift for you too, Mary Ann," Sandy says. She offered to take the first shift of driving, and most likely change drivers once they reach the Canada/U.S. border at Regway, Montana. But right at this moment, she wishes she wasn't at the wheel. She would much rather be watching her little sister open her package. It's official. Sandy has traditionally adopted Mary Ann, who she still calls Betsy every now and then.

"This is absolutely beautiful Sandy," Mary Ann says and

begins to tear-up as she holds a gorgeous satin dance shawl which sports the longest pink fringes she's ever seen.

"I wanted you to come out in style when we hit the dance floor. And those are your colours. Purple, the colour of majesty. Red, the colour of love. White indicating purity and innocence. And pink because we are girls." The shawl is adorned with an intricate appliqué of a hummingbird, which Sandy spent hours and hours hand-stitching and embroidering with golden thread.

Sandy explains why she chose this design. "You've always been attracted to hummingbirds and they to you." It's also because the hummingbird is symbolic of joyful memory. She knows that while there has been tragedy and loss in Mary Ann's life, the hummingbird is a reminder that life is short. "The little bird teaches us to make every moment count. To love and be loved and then love some more."

Sandy also made sure to embroider the image of a dancing raven on the shawl. "Kisakihtin Nimis."

Mary Ann blows a kiss in Sandy's direction. "I love you, too, my little sister."

"Awww. You guys are too much," Maynard calls the mood. "You're making me cry."

"Oh stop." Charlene then asks Maynard to hand her one of the sandwiches he's prepared.

"We'll work on the rest of your outfit when we get back from the Gathering of Nations," Sandy says to Mary Ann. "I will sew you a new dress. Charlene's been learning to make moccasins since Nina's been holding classes at the shelter lately. And I will bead you a yoke. But for now, your basic outfit will do just fine in Albuquerque. I am just so proud that you are dancing. Women's Fancy. Twirling like the wind. Nimihiowi Kakakiw Iskwew. "

"And, I can make you some earrings," Shad proposes.

"Oh yes, Mr. Shad. A gift for you too." Sandy knows it's important to invite him into the family. He's brought such happiness to Maynard. Maybe someday she'll call him a brother-in-law. But for now, she's just thankful he's a cherished friend. Shad's package reveals a colourful ribbon shirt. "The blue matches your eyes," Maynard notices.

As they near the Village of Ceylon near the Saskatchewan/Montana border, Sandy can't help but comment on a massive stone Inukshuk that a farmer has erected in his field. The stone beacon is common in the High Arctic. Fishers place the figure of a stone man along the coastline. The Inukshuk points to the way back home. But this is not something you'd necessarily expect to see in rural Saskatchewan.

The way back home, Sandy thinks and smiles. She offers a silent prayer of gratitude, before saying, "The only thing that would make this trip more perfect would be if Joe and Nina could have come too."

"Hiy, hiy," is the response from Amos. It's the first time in a decade that his dad, old Joe Bush Sr. hasn't made the trek to the Gathering of Nations. But the reason for his absence is a valid one.

Nina and Joe are not coming because they have been invited to speak at an Elder's Gathering out at Standing Buffalo, a picturesque Aboriginal community nestled along the shores of Pasqua Lake in Saskatchewan's scenic Qu'Appelle Valley. The topic is fake shamanism. But how can anyone know who is real and who is just pretending?

That important gathering was called because the local Tribal Council felt it necessary to talk about this ever since an ad was placed in the classified section of Regina's *LeaderPost* newspaper. The advertisement offers a course in *How To Be an Aboriginal Healer,* and states there are ten spots available. The fee to enroll for the one-month course is eleven-hundred dollars. Once instruction is completed, participants receive a certificate indicating they are a healer.

Nina agreed to watch Misty while the entourage makes their way to New Mexico. She laughed watching her six children—as she now refers to everyone—pack themselves into the rented passenger van. "You should just have rented a Winnebago," she jests, "that way you wouldn't have to worry about finding a hotel for you all."

The sun is almost setting as the gaggle of friends and family near a sign in the State of Wyoming. It points to Devil's Tower Mountain. It is a location prominent in the movie, *Close Encounters of the Third Kind*. Visiting the site is something Maynard has dreamed of. "I've always wanted to see this up close, Sandy. Feel the earth under my feet. We have to stop and remember this beautiful moment in time." With that, Maynard retrieves another cardboard disposable camera from his jacket pocket.

Sandy is tired and just wants to get to Albuquerque. Still she agrees to stop, so long as everyone stops calling the place Devil's Tower. She prefers to call it what the local Native people call it: Bear Lodge Butte. It is part of the Black Hills and a place where spirit is alive and the land speaks to those who wander and ponder and give thanks to this glory we call life.

Maybe they will even catch a glimpse of Bushman while here? Seems likely. Sandy notices some odd-looking tracks as she opens her vehicle door and smells the wind that holds a scent of history, battle, and pride.

She stands up and looks around her. Instead, she feels as though she has come home, and she realizes that is home is where you make it. It's not a place. It's all around you, so long as what is around you includes love and sunshine and family.

Sandy knows this because just at that moment she notices a tiny dogwood flower poking its head out between a crack in a boulder. And, she whispers the words, *Kisakihithin, Kohkum. Kinanaskomitin.*

ACKNOWLEDGEMENTS

In the writing of these words, I give special hugs to My Baby Bears: Jackson, Nahanni, and Daniel. You are my rock and my purpose. Love y'all more than words can ever express. You have grown so beautifully—like the dogwood—and I continue to say prayers that you flourish and grow and create beauty.

Thank you also to Neal McLeod, Janice Lentowicz, Brenda Montgrand, Gertie Montgrand, John Merasty, Angie Merasty, Cathy Wheaton, Solomon Ratt, Kenneth T. Williams, Cristian Moya, Squaw'kin Iskwewak Drum Group—Jamie Goulet, Dr. Wanda Wuttunee, and Wendy Prince-Moore—Elder Mae Louise Campbell, Nina Wilson, Joely BigEagle-Keequatooway, Lori Bradford, Kathy Butler, Kathy and Marc Barbeau, Leif Mehlsen, Stacey Fayant, Erik Mehlsen, John Kennedy, Bruce Spence, Kari Lentowicz, Mo Parent, Shane Turgeon, Brenda Pander-Stowe, Kala Montgrand, Dean Bernier, Brian Sklar, Autumn EagleSpeaker, Sandra Topinka, Karen Wheeler, Eunice Cameron, Carol Draper, Krista Hannan, Lori Zak, Desarae Eashappie, Betty Sellers, James Misfeldt, Jenny Matts, Pamela Cochet, Duane and Carol Wright, Kristin Teetaert, Georgina and Ross Carter, Bernadette Wagner, Kristin Catherwood, Ruth Barker Veronica and Glen Lucas, Leah Blink, Norma Littlechild, Melissa Stoops, Grant Lawrence, Anna Boyar, Tracey George Hesse, Joan Halberg-Mayer, Colleen Marcotte, Vi and Victor Thunderchild, Tyler Walker, Vanessa Matechuk, Jennifer and

Jesse Schneider, Jenny Kriekle, and all of my amazing friends at the Beach.

And this may sound odd, but I also thank my dog, Saffy, because I get so many ideas while I am out walking and she makes me walk each and every day.

And, it goes without saying, much gratitude to Creator, the Angels, and my own Spirit Helpers who help me to create and keep me safe.

Also thank you to so many others, if I have forgotten you on this list. Always remember you are in my heart. Namaste. Sending love.

Special acknowledgement goes to the Saskatchewan Arts Board for its generous support of this project.

Finally, thank you to Inanna Publications.